CU00853473

THE ABBEY OF

DEATH

A Forest Lord novella

by

STEVEN A. MCKAY

ALSO BY STEVEN A. MCKAY

The Forest Lord Series:

Wolf's Head

The Wolf and the Raven

Rise of the Wolf

Blood of the Wolf

Knight of the Cross

Friar Tuck and the Christmas Devil

The Rescue And Other Tales

COMING SOON

The Druid

Summer 1328, Selby Abbey

The pleasant sound of a dozen male voices working in harmony rose to fill the great vaulted chamber, proclaiming the glory of God and His creation, and Will Scaflock felt his spirits lift as if carried up by the power of the music.

He wasn't much of a singer and self-consciously kept his own voice a little quieter than his Benedictine brothers, but he was getting better, and every so often he'd feel real pleasure upon realising he was actually hitting the same note as the rest of the choir.

The cantor, John de Loup, had despaired of Will when he'd first come to join them at Selby Abbey a few months earlier, but the choirmaster would take any new recruit he could find. Although there were thirty-five monks in the abbey, only a third of them ever bothered coming to practice. God knew where the others were.

Actually, the cantor knew very well where many of the missing monks were and so did Will. The former outlaw had been surprised to find so many of his new brothers being censured often by the abbot for a variety of transgressions against the Rule of Saint Benedict: sending alms meant for the Church to women they favoured, stealing, public drunkenness, even fornication.

Archbishop Melton of York had visited just a few years ago and demanded Abbot de Wystow bring the miscreants into line, but the truth was, the ageing cleric was too soft-hearted to provide the discipline demanded by his superior.

Admittedly, things were not as lax as they'd been at the archbishop's last visit – or so Brother Nicholas de

Houghton, a young man who'd befriended Will, attested. Nicholas himself had been one of the worst offenders a couple of years ago, but he'd calmed down ever since his twenty-first birthday and become a productive, popular member of the brethren.

Still, there were half a dozen or so monks who continued to ignore the abbot's demands for stricter observance of the Rule. Will had nearly come to blows with a few of them in the months he'd been here but, somehow, had managed to restrain himself.

He'd joined the Benedictines to leave that life behind, after all – to find peace in prayer and contemplation. He would never have believed it a decade ago if someone had told him he'd be a monk by the time he was forty-two, yet here he was. Singing, mostly out of tune, in the choir.

The song died away, and silence filled the high-ceilinged chamber with its wooden arches as the cantor looked out at them from the lectern, a small smile on his round face.

'Glory be to God,' Brother de Loup muttered, laying down his hymnal and raising his arms theatrically. 'That was rather good. Even Brother Scaflock managed to remain in tune for some of it. Off you go then.' He gestured at the monks to be about their work, exhorting them to practise while they swept or baked or copied or whatever else they might be employed in that afternoon.

'Not you, Brother Scaflock. I'd like a word if you don't mind.'

Will had already begun to walk out of the choir with the rest of the chattering monks – he had gardening to do and genuinely looked forward to the physical labour which had always been part of his life – but he turned now, eyebrows raised. Had his singing been so bad that he needed one-to-one tuition?

'Don't look so worried.' The cantor smiled as he crossed the floor to lower his bulk into the sedilia, a short row of stone seats that were carved into the wall. 'Come, sit with me. I just wanted to know how you're settling in.'

Will took a seat next to de Loup gratefully, although the stone was uncomfortably cold. Even in late summer the abbey rarely felt warm inside, so although sunshine peered through the stained-glass windows, the choir remained quite chilly.

The cantor, with his portly frame, jovial face and twinkling eyes, always reminded Will of his old friend Friar Tuck, and he knew the cold seat would soon warm. He would sit a while with de Loup, and gladly.

'Aye, I'm doing well enough.' The one-time wolf's head and member of Robin Hood's legendary gang nodded. 'It's not the most exciting life but I'm well fed, there's enough ale and the work keeps me fit.'

The cantor knew much of Scaflock's history because the abbot had told him. He knew the well-built, green-eyed man had once been a mercenary before becoming the outlaw known as Will Scarlet when his family were massacred by a former employer. Although he didn't talk about it, and no one asked, it was common knowledge that his family's murderers had suffered the same bloody fate at Will's own hands.

The man was – or had been – a violent killer, but when Robin Hood's gang won their pardons from King Edward II, Will had settled down to life as a peaceful farmer before, for reasons of his own, finding his way to Selby Abbey where he'd become a Benedictine monk.

And he was a good monk, working hard and participating in prayers and hymns, even if he did become moody or angry at times.

'I'm happy to see you finding some pleasure in our simple life.' De Loup nodded, clasping Will by the shoulder in an almost fatherly way. 'If you ever feel like you want to talk to someone, you know where I am. I'm sure you find it hard being away from your daughter and her baby.'

Will's face creased with a mix of emotions at the mention of Beth. She'd grown up now, and started a family of her own, and there seemed little need for him in their lives. Loneliness had driven him to the Benedictines, but thinking of his daughter, and grandson Robert, brought joy to his heart.

Until he inevitably remembered all the loved ones he'd lost over the years. His wife, Elaine, and their sons Matthew and David. Not to mention the many friends he'd seen killed during his time as an outlaw.

Maybe he would talk to Brother de Loup about the crushing loneliness he felt; one day, soon.

For now he had weeds to clear and seeds to plant.

* * *

Two weeks later Will was outside in the garden again, ripping up weeds and filling a wheelbarrow with them as birdsong filled the abbey grounds. He was helped by his young friend, Brother Nicholas, and they worked well together, although small talk was kept to a minimum. Still, Will felt a true bond of friendship with the lad, who was pious and devoted to God even if he'd been something of a rebel in his past.

Tall and strong, despite the slight limp that was the legacy of a childhood accident, Brother Nicholas de

Houghton had truly put his womanising days behind him, and Will saw a lot of himself in the younger man.

They were sweating in the warm air, enjoying their task beneath the sunshine, when the abbot appeared, wandering through the garden with a paternal smile on his long, thin face. The monks he passed nodded deferentially to him and redoubled their efforts, cheered by his approval of their labours. Abbot John de Wystow II was a good man, Will thought, but he didn't have the steel in him to be a truly great leader.

The grounds were large and surrounded by a high stone wall encompassing the chapel, cloisters, stables, brewhouse, kitchen, workshops, dormitory, infirmary, and various minor buildings.

'Oh-ho,' Will muttered when he noticed the three men who'd just stumbled through the huge gatehouse and were heading along the path straight for the abbot, oblivious in their obvious drunkenness to his presence.

We'll see now whether he's a strong leader or not.

Nicholas paused from hauling up the roots of some brambles and wiped his brow with a grimy sleeve as he heard the inebriated monks coming towards them, then he spat on the freshly turned earth.

'Brother Robert,' Will heard the abbot say, the old man's voice high-pitched but strong. 'And your two friends, Brothers Thomas and John. What is the meaning of this? Haven't you three been warned often enough?' He strode right up to the trio of tipsy monks, who eyed one another like naughty schoolboys, and Will had to restrain himself as he felt an almost overwhelming urge to go across and teach the fools some respect.

But he held himself in check, watching from lowered brows as Abbot de Wystow lectured the drunks. It wasn't

Will's place to sort out discipline in the abbey – he was simply Brother Scaflock now, no longer Will Scarlet, lieutenant to Robin Hood. Yet he couldn't help watching as the confrontation proceeded.

'Well? Answer me!' the abbot cried. 'Look there. Your brothers are working hard tending the garden while you three have been out visiting Selby's taverns from the look – and smell – of it.' He screwed up his face and wafted a bony hand in front of his nose as if to dispel the alcoholic fumes issuing from the drunken monks' mouths. 'Never mind. You're clearly in no state to understand me. We shall talk in the morning and you can be sure there will be repercussions for your disgusting behaviour.'

He gestured and the three monks walked past hurriedly, heads bowed as if in remorse, although their faces told a different story. Their eyes were wide and one of them even held his nose as if he might explode into laughter at any moment, but they somehow managed to put a safe distance between themselves and Abbot de Wystow before muffled sniggers escaped their lips.

Their leader was a very tall, middle-aged man called Robert de Flexburgh, and he strode along in front of his two younger companions, Thomas de Hirst and John de Whitgift, an arrogant, haughty look on his seamed face. He caught sight of Brother Nicholas staring as they came closer, and his brow furrowed.

'Don't you look at me like that, you little prick. You're no better than any of us. You were out screwing that lass of yours like she was a whore for long enough, before you turned all pious.'

'Wouldn't mind a go on her myself,' de Whitgift, a small, handsome monk with fine white teeth, leered from behind his mentor.

Will looked on with interest, wondering what his friend would do in the face of the drunks' provocation, but to his credit, Nicholas remained silent, simply glaring murderously at his tormentors.

As is ever the way with bullies though, de Flexburgh didn't appreciate being ignored, and he walked across to the wheelbarrow Nicholas and Will had been using to gather their weeds for the past quarter of an hour.

The big, red-faced monk grabbed the handle of the barrow and, with a furious, challenging glare at Brother Nicholas, tipped its contents out onto the earth.

Will placed a hand firmly on his friend's shoulder and gently pulled him back before the young monk could launch himself at the powerfully built troublemaker.

Brother de Flexburgh noticed Will's intervention and his eyes grew even harder. Clearly alcohol made the man an angry, violent drunk, rather than a happy one, as his two ale-soaked companions appeared to be. Brothers de Whitgift and de Hirst both stood back, watching the confrontation gleefully, sensing their friend was about to deal out a beating.

Will shook his head in confusion. He knew people well enough – he'd spent many years dealing with all kinds after all, from murderers and rapists to mercenaries who killed for pleasure as much as for silver, to good friends who'd give up their own life to protect their companions. And yet it still baffled him that monks would behave like this. If they wanted to live a life of vice, why didn't they leave the order?

Because they have it easy here, an inner voice told him. They have comfortable lodgings, plentiful meat and drink, and an abbot that lets them act however they please, even protecting them from the law.

'Ah, it's the old wolf's head,' de Flexburgh growled, stepping close, and Will could understand why Abbot de Wystow had tried to wave the smell away. The monk reeked of strong drink, although his eyes were clear enough. 'Sorry, wolf's head. I spilled all your weeds onto the ground.'

'Oops!' one of his two friends mumbled from the back, and the three of them sniggered drunkenly.

'Well, you'd better pick them up then, hadn't you?' Will replied in a soft voice, and it was young Brother Nicholas's turn to step back and watch proceedings with interest.

'What?' De Flexburgh seemed stunned that anyone would stand up to him and he leaned back, seeming to grow in his surprise, but Will had dealt with much bigger and much deadlier foes than this fool in his time.

'I said you'd better pick up that pile of weeds that me and Brother Nicholas have just collected, and put them back in the wheelbarrow, you sweaty turd.' Will smiled, but his relaxed stance was completely at odds with his tone, and his taller opponent seemed utterly bemused by the whole situation.

For years Brother Robert de Flexburgh had behaved however he liked, pushing the monks of Selby Abbey around, and here was this newcomer, a notorious criminal, giving him orders? Before he could lash out, Will broke in again.

'I said pick them up, Brother, before I grind your face into the ground amongst them.'

De Hirst and De Whitgift hooted in sheer delight at the former outlaw's threat, knowing now that a fight was inevitable. They glanced at one another, eyes sparkling, from amusement as much as from the drink, and waited to see what would happen.

If their leader was winning, they'd join in with a few kicks of their own. Looking at Will Scaflock, though, neither of them were sure if de Flexburgh would come out on top as he usually did.

Before the big, brutish monk could turn his rage and astonishment into movement, Will's right hand exploded upwards and the hard muscle of his palm connected with de Flexburgh's chin, knocking the man's head back with a jarring click of teeth. Continuing his momentum, Will stretched his leg out and hooked it behind his opponent's ankle, dragging it towards him so de Flexburgh crashed to the ground with an outraged cry, blood spilling from his mouth where he'd bitten the tip of his tongue.

Will's smile was gone now and he glared at the onlookers, silently daring them to help their friend. Both de Hirst and de Whitgift were too frightened to move though, stunned by the speed and ferocity of the new monk's attack. Neither man had ever seen a fight start or end so quickly.

'Saints above,' Brother Nicholas muttered from behind Will. 'That was wonderful.'

The fallen drunk, head well and truly mashed into the weeds he'd tipped onto the grass, groaned and turned a baleful eye on his attacker. 'I'll make your life a living hell for that,' he promised, but Will waved away the words.

'I'm still waiting on you to pick those weeds up.'

'Damn your weeds,' de Flexburgh cried, wiping the blood from his chin with the back of his hand and staring at it in outrage. 'And damn you—'

His two companions knew enough was enough, for now, and each grasped one of the big man's arms, hauling him back before he could engage Will in a proper fight. The old wolf's head's calm demeanour made the monks nervous and de Flexburgh, although he raged and flailed, was clearly not trying very hard to break free of his friends' restraining grip.

He was well beaten, but his eyes promised revenge on another day.

Will was somewhat surprised by the worried looks on de Hirst and de Whitgift's faces as they eyed their bloodied friend – clearly they liked de Flexburgh well enough. Maybe the man had some redeeming qualities after all.

'Next time you piss me off, or annoy my friend Brother Nicholas here, I'll give you more than a bloody mouth,' Will growled, as the defeated trio moved off like some localised whirlwind that had lost most of its power. He looked round at Nicholas and a grin spread across his face which the younger man couldn't help sharing, before shouting a final, sarcastic barb.

'Go in peace, my brothers!'

* * *

A week went by and none of the bullies paid much heed to either Will or Nicholas, and Scaflock began to wonder if the men had been more drunk than he'd thought. Had they forgotten all about the altercation in the garden? Or were they simply biding their time?

Will didn't particularly care. He'd spent years of his life looking over his shoulder, ready for death – it was a habit he'd never lose now. He would be ready for de Flexburgh and his lackeys if they came for him. He'd thought about following his old friend Friar Tuck's example and secreting a cudgel beneath his black robe, but finally rejected the idea. He'd left the life of an armed fighter behind – if someone wanted to attack him he'd use only the tools God had given him to defend himself.

'Did you hear all that shouting at the gates last night?' Brother Nicholas whispered as they ate their midday meal in the chilly refectory while, according to St Benedict's Rule, one of the brothers was reading aloud from some old text. Meals were supposed to be eaten in silence, listening to the reader, but Abbot de Wystow was rather lax in enforcing the regulations.

Will shook his head and spooned some of the pottage into his mouth. The dormitory was at the rear of the building, on the opposite side from the front gate.

'What was it all about?' he asked, in a similar low tone.

Nicholas glanced to his left, eyes taking in the laughing figure of Brother de Flexburgh at the far end of the long table, and leaned in conspiratorially. 'Him and his mates have been annoying the townsfolk again.'

Will looked along the table and pursed his lips in disgust when he saw whom his friend was talking about.

'Some of the folk were at the gate after dark last night, shouting for the abbot. Demanding he do something about discipline here in the abbey. Or else.' He ended in a harsh whisper, face flushed with anxiety.

'Or else?' Will mumbled, still shoving food into his mouth. He'd spent another hard morning in the garden watering the vegetables and shovelling manure onto the earth to help them grow, and it had worked up a fine appetite. 'Or else what?'

Brother Nicholas shrugged, but the monk's simple gesture was heavy with portent and Will felt a shiver of anxiety run down his back. He looked sideways again at de Flexburgh, who was leading an obnoxiously loud conversation amongst his followers, drawing disapproving looks from many of the older monks including the cantor.

De Flexburgh and the rest of his company finally finished their meal and left the room, leaving their used bowls and cups on the table for someone else to clean up.

Will noticed de Loup's hard eyes following the troublesome lot until they were gone, but then the cantor turned and gazed right at Scaflock and his expression darkened even further.

'What are you doing now?' Nicholas asked, oblivious to De Loup's black look in their direction. 'We have a little free time until Nones . No doubt de Flexburgh and his mates are heading off into town to see their lady friends. I'd suggest we stay well clear given the mood in Selby. Might be trouble.'

Will shrugged and rose from the table, taking his empty bowl and ale-mug over to the kitchen to wash them out. 'I expect the abbot has had a word with those fools. The man might be soft-hearted but he's not soft in the head. He won't want an angry mob coming here – word would soon reach the archbishop.' He shoved his dishes into the lukewarm water in the stone basin, wiped the remnants of his food away, and then used one of the rags to dry them off before placing them back on the shelves in one of the cupboards. 'I think I'll just go into the garden and find a quiet spot to pray for a while – these walls stifle me at times.'

Brother Nicholas put his own clean dish and mug back in their places and followed Will back out, through the refectory and into the sunshine. It was a fine, scorching hot day, a true blessing from God, yet the young monk sensed a melancholy in his friend. A sadness that clung to the former outlaw like a heavy cloak.

'Would you like me to join you?'

'No!'

Will glared at him, then his hard, lined face softened and he shook his head. 'Thank you, lad, but I'd rather be alone with God for a while.'

Nicholas watched his friend go, head bowed, shoulders slumped, and he hoped Will would find the peace he deserved.

* * *

Will sat, head bowed, on an old tree stump in a secluded area of the large gardens, the broad leaves of a young beech offering him some protection from the sunshine. His hands were clasped and he had the vacant expression of someone deep in meditation, and yet he felt a little guilty.

He'd told Brother Nicholas he was coming here to pray, and he often did come to this place where he knew he'd not be disturbed, but he never prayed, not really. Not like the devout monks – the ones that wore hair shirts and scourged themselves bloody in the name of God – did.

No, Will came to reminisce. Sometimes he would think about his wife and children who'd been slaughtered so horribly when he was a much younger man, and how different his life might have been had they lived. Those thoughts always made him angry, but then he'd remember his daughter Beth – who had survived that brutal, murderous day – and he would wonder in confusion whether to thank God or to rage at Him.

He had found happiness and contentment in life when he'd been pardoned a few years ago and begun living on his farm with Beth. But since his girl had married and moved to her new family home, even though she was still within Wakefield, he'd found himself increasingly morose and lonely. Work on the farm came to bore him, and he'd wondered what the point of it all was. Surely he was just passing the days in meaningless, worthless toil until, eventually, he'd meet his dead family in Heaven.

Of his old friends from Robin Hood's gang he only saw Tuck around town, but the friar was a busy man doing God's work. Little John would very occasionally visit from his blacksmith's workshop in Holderness, but Stephen had rejoined his beloved Hospitallers. Thomas L'Archer, the old Grand Prior who had held the grudge against him, was near to death and a replacement already lined up – Leonard de Tybertis had assumed command in all but name and he was friendly to Stephen, knowing him from years earlier. So the bluff Hospitaller sergeant had left for service in Rhodes, and Will's other old friends like Peter and Arthur were all either moved to far-off places or simply dead.

When Beth had given birth to his grandson, Will had been both proud and overjoyed. But it only made his solitary existence on the farm feel even lonelier, as he'd recall his younger days with his wife when they'd looked after their own beautiful babies.

Tears spilled down his cheeks and he didn't bother to wipe them away.

When Tuck suggested he become a monk it had seemed like a crazy idea at first. After all, Will had never been very religious. And yet that was the thing that decided him in the end: maybe God could replace his family, and Jesus would fill the gaping wound in his soul. It seemed to have worked for Tuck, who was a generally happy, contented man, which was all Will hoped for.

It was either that or, at past forty years of age, become a mercenary again, and the thought of killing strangers for money now seemed repugnant. He was past that, for better or worse.

Strangely enough – horribly enough! – his previous life as a sell-sword seemed to live on in his memory as some of the best times he'd ever had. A young, hard man learning to fight, to crush his enemies as part of a powerful army, drinking and carousing with his loyal companions . . .

All these images from his life spun around in his head and he felt as though he might go mad.

He raised his tear-streaked face to the sky and silently wondered, again, what the hell was the point of it all?

This wasn't the life for him.

When Brother de Flexburgh and his arsehole friends acted like spoiled noble lordlings, he wanted nothing more than to beat the crap out of them. That wasn't how a man of God – a Benedictine monk – should think, though. He knew de Flexburgh's lackeys felt great affection for him, so clearly the man wasn't quite the black monster he appeared to be in Will's head. Who knew what hardships the big monk had suffered in his life to make him the person he was now? That was how a true man of God should look at the situation.

Will had no place in the abbey and should never have come.

Should he?

Again, his mind whirled and he told himself he had to persevere – to work harder at his relationship with God if he wanted to find peace either here or in the afterlife.

Surely he was in Selby for a reason.

Gravel crunched on the path close by and he hurriedly wiped his face with the hem of his habit, glad the warm sun had dried his tears by now, although he was sure his eyes must still be red and puffy.

The cantor, Brother de Loup, appeared, walking slowly past the sweetly scented rosemary and lavender bushes and heading for Will as if he'd known he was there.

'Brother.' Will nodded in greeting, somewhat warily, knowing from the way the man had come straight towards him that this was no chance encounter.

'I see your windflowers are still doing well,' the cantor said, taking a seat next to him and pointing at a small patch of white blooms nearby. 'They don't usually flower as late as this; you've tended them well.'

'With your help.' Will nodded, smiling, remembering the day his friendship with the cantor had truly been cemented.

One of his biggest frustrations as a farmer had been his inability to grow certain plants. Vegetables were simple enough, but he had always wanted to add some colour to his land, particularly around the house, to brighten the place up for Beth. When he'd noticed some pretty white flowers with a musky smell in the garden of his widower friend, Elspeth, he'd asked to take some and she'd happily helped him dig a few out and replant them.

They had never taken properly though, despite his careful tending, and it upset him, making him think more than ever that he was better suited to killing than nurturing life.

Then he'd come to the abbey and noticed a small patch of those same flowers growing here in this quiet part of the garden. They'd been well past their flowering cycle by then, and Will resolved to nurture them as best he could when they were reborn the following spring. But when the time came, despite his best efforts, they were limp and stunted when they should have been blooming. And then Brother de Loup had come upon him, just as he had today, and noticed his sad expression.

'Those are windflowers,' the cantor had told him. 'They need a certain kind of soil if they're to reach their full potential. I thought you were a farmer before?'

Will had been too interested to be angry at the question, especially when de Loup headed back into the abbey, returning a short time later with a cup of vinegar.

'Add a little of this every time you water the flowers.'

Will had thought the old monk mad – vinegar! – but he had followed the advice and, well, the results were plain for all to see, as the small white flowers now filled the air around them with the musky scent that reminded him fondly of his friend Elspeth.

He had been so thankful for the cantor's help and felt he should repay the man, even if it was just with his friendship.

'I heard about you beating Brother de Flexburgh,' de Loup said unexpectedly, bringing him back to the present, and Will felt like a child receiving a telling-off from a parent, his face flushing red, friendly thoughts gone.

'The bastard deserved it and more.'

'Did you know he bit off the end of his tongue?'

Will shrugged. 'Five years ago I'd have left him in a much worse state. Trust me, he deserved what he got, and more.'

De Loup nodded. 'I completely agree,' he said, surprisingly. 'If I was the abbot, and had your fighting skills, I'd thrash the man and set an example to the foolish boys that follow him around.'

'So why the dark looks?' Will asked, sensing a 'but' in the cantor's words.

'It is not your place to teach these men discipline, Brother Scaflock.'

There was a silence for a time then, as both men watched each other grimly. De Loup finally went on, his voice lower, less harsh this time.

'You came to us to escape a life of conflict, and to find peace. Let Abbot de Wystow run the abbey the way he sees fit – trust me, he's not as weak as he appears. He might even surprise you one day. Tend your windflowers and the rest of the garden. Work on your singing. Pray! And, if you feel the need, come to me to talk about your purpose in life or your fears. Please – you'll find I have a sympathetic ear.'

He smiled, and again Will was struck by the man's resemblance to Friar Tuck. It wasn't in the way he looked so much as his manner, and Will found himself returning the smile gratefully.

'Furthermore,' the cantor continued, his face growing hard again. 'Next time you get into a fight with that oaf de Flexburgh, make sure you take the whole tongue off the noisy bastard, not just the tip.'

Will burst out laughing and the tension between them dissipated completely. They were kindred spirits these two, despite their vastly different paths through life.

The companionable silence was suddenly disturbed by the sound of shouts and running feet, and Will jumped up, force of habit making him reach for a sword that wasn't there anymore.

'Close the gates! Close the gates now, or we're all dead men!'

The voices finally came close enough to make out and the cantor also got to his feet, although with none of Will's nimbleness.

'De Flexburgh again, from the sounds of it,' de Loup sighed irritably. 'Come on, you might as well come with me and see what the hell he, and his useless friends, have done now.'

As they hurried towards the front entrance, Will wished he hadn't rejected the idea of carrying a club, as the babble of many angry, threatening voices could be heard descending upon the abbey.

It sounded as though the people of Selby had finally had enough of the wayward monks.

* * *

As Will and the cantor headed towards the gates, the tall, lean figure of Abbot de Wystow could be seen ahead of them; just as he reached the entry to the abbey grounds, Brother de Flexburgh came charging past, breathless and wide-eyed, although Will noted a strange gleam in his eyes before he disappeared into the great stone building.

Will could see the main road leading towards their gates now, and coming towards the abbey was a mob of possibly twenty or thirty people, all moving at as fast a pace as they could manage. Abbot de Wystow stopped to glare out at them defiantly however, straight-backed and confident.

The cantor muttered an unseemly curse and hurried ahead to stand beside the abbot, while Will, mindful of his lack of status within the abbey, stood back at a respectful distance, his battle-hardened eyes taking in the oncoming mob. It appeared to be nothing more than some irate townsfolk – he could see a baker, clearly marked by the flour dusting his apron, and a black-bearded butcher with similarly stained garb, although his sported a bloody livery of crimson and brown rather than clean white.

It seemed a rabble, and yet Will's long years of experience told him something was amiss. He stared out, searching, until he noticed the men on the far left of the approaching mob, just behind the butcher. Half a dozen of them, these men had a certain look about them which Will knew immediately, for he'd seen it often enough: soldiers.

They wore no livery, instead blending into the crowd almost seamlessly in grubby brown gambesons and breeches. Not quite soldiers – they surely had been at one point, but now those six men were more than likely outlaws.

Why would a gang of wolf's heads join an angry mob? Did they seek to plunder the abbey in the commotion? Again Will wished he had a weapon of some sort, as he knew those hard-eyed men would certainly be armed.

Four of de Flexburgh's friends appeared and sprinted in through the gates, drawing an angry glare from the abbot, but the terrified men didn't slow and were soon lost from view inside the church.

As he watched, Will spotted a final, lone, black-robed monk still struggling along the road towards the abbey: Brother Adam de la Breuer. At thirty-five the man was almost as old as de Flexburgh, but he clearly didn't have the stamina or turn of speed his friend boasted and he lagged behind, panting like a thirsty dog, the skin on his scalp almost as red as the untidy ginger hair around his tonsure.

'What is the meaning of this?' Abbot de Wystow demanded, his voice strong and powerful, but the approaching mob paid him no heed as their quarry seemed to catch his foot on some invisible obstacle, then, almost in slow motion, stumble for half a dozen paces before sprawling flat on his face with a cry of fear.

Some of the other Benedictines had come out from the church to see what was happening and they all stood there now, watching in horrified silence – cantor and abbot among them – as the forerunners of the mob caught up to the fallen de la Breuer and began to beat him savagely.

Will looked on, surprised at the violence the townspeople were doling out towards a clergyman, but he wasn't inclined to go to the fallen monk's aid. Brother de la Breuer was, in Will's opinion, an arsehole. A drunk and a troublemaker, the monk had been accused of having carnal knowledge of not just Alice, the smith's daughter, but her sister too. If the mob wanted to deal out some justice with their fists and feet, well, de la Breuer surely deserved it.

The ginger-tonsured monk wasn't any better liked by the other Benedictines who looked on impassively as he was kicked and punched, squealing loudly but not even attempting to defend himself.

Abbot de Wystow, however, was a different matter.

'That's enough!' he roared, striding out through the relative safety of the gates towards the enraged mob, who, having started on a path of violence, clearly felt there was no going back.

A rock sailed overhead, silently, just missing the abbot, and the man flinched. Apparently he hadn't expected to be attacked, but in this he was sorely mistaken, as another rock flew past, then another, before at last, inevitably, one bounced off de Wystow's lean frame and sent him reeling, a pained look on his face.

Will knew something wasn't right about this whole situation and he couldn't just stand back and do nothing any longer. The mob had continued their beating of Brother de la Breuer, but some of them, intoxicated with aggression and their sense of righteous retribution, ran ahead now, eyes fixed on the fallen abbot while yet others headed for the shocked cantor.

Will saw the men he'd marked as soldiers hanging back, not joining the mad charge, and, planning to mount a defence, he spun to glare at the monks standing shocked and indecisive at his back. His heart sank at how few there were – just eleven of them, and half their number over fifty years of age. It was hardly a fighting force to be reckoned with, but it was all he had.

'What are you waiting for?' he roared, his powerful voice filling the muggy air. 'Defend your brothers – follow me!'

Will turned back and began to run out, through the gates, making straight for the abbot, who was lying curled up in a ball in the road now as blows rained down upon him; and, once more, Will desperately wished he hadn't rejected the idea of carrying a club. Realistically, without a weapon he could hope to incapacitate only three or four – five at a push – of the attackers. It wouldn't be enough, especially once the outlaws at the back of the mob joined in with the assault.

Even so, he had to defend the abbot, and he charged recklessly towards the boiling mass, half of him frightened to be going into battle without a weapon in his hand, the other half overjoyed at this day's excitement after the staid, boring existence of months locked inside Selby Abbey.

But even Will Scarlet couldn't stand against a fist-sized rock when it tore through the air and smashed into his face.

* * *

Sounds came to him as if through a thick fog that blanketed his head.

Sad, low voices with the occasional creak of smashed wood or clatter of something being tossed onto a pile.

With a sudden flash of clarity Will remembered what had happened, and his eyes half opened so he could survey the situation.

Were his brother monks all dead? Were the sounds coming from the victorious townspeople, was their anger satiated and remorse – and fear of the law – overcoming their earlier fury?

Years of instinct made his hand move slowly to his waist, but his sword was long gone and he cursed inwardly.

'You're all right!' A voice, filled with relief, came from his right and he turned, eyes fully open, to peer at Brother Nicholas, who seemed uninjured and gratifyingly pleased to find his friend alive and awake. 'I was worried that rock might have addled your brain. It didn't, did it?'

'No.' Will waved a hand weakly and pulled himself up on the wooden bench someone had placed him on. 'I'm fine, I think. Just got a bastard of a headache.' He looked around the room, noting it was the infirmary that he'd been brought to, and was surprised to see no obvious damage.

'The mob didn't come this far inside the precincts,' Nicholas said. 'Thankfully there weren't that many of them, so their fury was quickly spent before they came to their senses and left. Some things were stolen from the presbytery and the chapel but it could have been worse. The noises you can hear are from the kitchen – that was ransacked too.'

'What about the abbot?'

'Alive, thank God, although he's in a worse state than you. He's old and took a bit of a beating . . .'

Will felt sick. Not from the head injury he'd suffered – that was nothing compared to the shame he felt at not defending the brothers who'd taken him into their fold.

Of all the men gathered in Selby Abbey, Will Scaflock was the one who should have been an asset in a fight. He should have led the defenders against the rampaging crowd, but instead he'd been taken out of the battle before it had even truly begun, and spent it lying on his back while the abbot and the other monks were beaten and humiliated and their possessions stolen.

Robin and Little John would have given him hell if they could see him now. He could picture their grinning faces and it only made him feel worse.

'I should have helped . . .'

'None of that,' Brother Nicholas said, shaking his head firmly. 'I can see the wheels turning in your head but you're not to blame for any of this, so don't start with any self-pity.' He smiled to offset his harsh words, and put out a hand to help Will to his feet. 'Come on. If you're feeling better you can help us tidy up the mess those heathen bastards left behind.'

The former wolf's head allowed himself to be lifted to his feet and he stood there feeling dizzy and nauseous, but the sensation eventually passed and he nodded gratefully to the younger monk, both for the physical help and the telling-off.

'Fine. Let's get to work then.'

They headed out and along the corridor towards the kitchen, which looked as if a whirlwind had hit it. While some of the members of the mob had looked for golden crucifixes, others simply wanted to carry off meat and ale. Cupboards had their doors torn off, despite the fact most of them hadn't even been locked, while cups, trenchers and pots were strewn around the floor, dented or smashed beyond repair.

'What kind of madness makes a man throw a cauldron against the wall?' Will muttered, taking in the sight in bemusement before grabbing some of the damaged items and tossing them into one of the wheelbarrows brought in to help with the clean-up. Then another, more important thought came to him through the fog that still clouded his head.

'Was anyone killed?'

Nicholas nodded, tossing half a splintered mug across the room into another barrow. 'Brother de la Breuer suffered quite a thrashing. He bore the brunt of the mob's fury after he fell in the road. De Flexburgh has been quite upset about it – they must have been better friends than I realised.' He shrugged and wiped sweat from his brow before bending to scoop up a dented goblet. 'If de Breuer hadn't been in his cups he'd never have stumbled and might have made it to safety like his friends did.'

Will stopped working and furrowed his brow. 'So an angry rabble attacked the abbey, but only one person was killed and all they did was steal a few things?'

'Aye. Truly God was at work here today, eh? We were lucky.'

Will suddenly recalled the out-of-place military-looking types who'd appeared to be with, yet were somehow separate from the rest of the mob, and wondered what part they'd played in the assault on the abbey. Damn it, if only he'd been conscious!

'Shame God didn't look after the cantor,' one of the other monks, overhearing their conversation, butted in, drawing surprised looks from both Will and Nicholas.

'The cantor?'

'Aye,' the monk, a haggard, middle-aged man with many laughter lines, replied. 'Brother de Loup was taken. I saw it myself.'

Will crossed to stand in front of the exhausted monk, all thoughts of tidying the mess gone from his head.

'What do you mean? Taken where? By whom?'

'No one knows where they took him, but I saw the men that did it. Hard-looking men they were – I didn't recognise any of them from the town, so mayhap they were strangers.' He shrugged and shook his head sadly. 'Who knows what they've done with de Loup.'

'Hasn't anyone gone looking for him?' Will demanded, anger turning his face red, and the haggard monk shrank back in alarm.

'Who would search for him? We're men of God, not soldiers or lawmen.'

Brother Nicholas stepped forward and interposed himself between the two men, raising his palms reassuringly.

'Do you know if anyone has sent word to Nottingham for the sheriff?'

'Yes, Brother Wilfred rode out an hour ago to report the news.' The haggard monk went back to cleaning the messy kitchen. 'Hopefully de Faucumberg sends a few of his soldiers to capture the animals that did this to our home.'

'That's no use,' Will railed, turning to push past the other monks hard at work and striding towards the abbot's quarters. 'The cantor will be dead by the time lawmen reach here from the city.'

Nicholas hurried after him, sandals slapping on the hard stone floor as he tried to catch up.

'What are you going to do?'

Will wasn't sure himself yet, so he walked on in silence. He felt he had to do something though – the cantor was one of only two men in Selby Abbey he could truly call a friend.

He wouldn't – couldn't – just stand around while the man was in the hands of those grim mercenaries.

* * *

Abbot de Wystow was still in a bad way, so Will and Brother Nicholas found his chambers barred by the small, competent figure of his deputy, Prior John Ousthorp. The man had no interest in talking to two of the lowest novices within the abbey, however, and he sent them on their way without answering any of Will's questions about the abbot's welfare or any possible search for the cantor.

Instead, the prior ordered them to help clear up the mess made by the invading mob, and to pray for the abbot's welfare. He appeared unconcerned about the cantor and Will guessed the two men weren't close friends.

There was nothing else for it – Brother Scaflock had to throw himself back into the task of restoring Selby Abbey to its former glory, whether he felt like it or not.

This was the life he'd chosen, and the prior, as the abbot's second-in-command, was now the man he had to take orders from.

For two more days Will busied himself with his work, Brother Nicholas at his side, both men growing increasingly alarmed at the continued absence of the cantor, while no help from Sheriff de Faucumberg, the coroner or even the bailiff was forthcoming. Rumour had it that the bailiff was away on other, more pressing, business and wouldn't be able to reach Selby for at least another week.

Will suspected the lawmen simply didn't want to get embroiled in affairs of the Church, but he was becoming distinctly impatient.

'Ah, bugger this,' he said to Nicholas on the third morning since Brother de Loup had been spirited away. The subdued atmosphere of the abbey had begun to grate badly on his nerves and he was fed up with the cold stone walls and the other monks' sad faces. 'We can't get past that pompous prior, and no one else seems interested in helping the cantor, so I'm going into town to see if I can find anything out for myself.'

'You can't do that,' his friend replied. 'We've been told not to leave the abbey grounds. Even de Flexburgh and his mates haven't ventured back into town, and you know they do whatever they please most of the time. The prior had the gates barred after all the trouble.'

'De Flexburgh is the one that caused all this – of course he hasn't been back into Selby. The people will probably string him up by the neck if they see him around again. But me?' He grinned disarmingly. 'The folk there don't really know me as a monk, but some of them might know me as Will Scarlet, the mythical wolf's head. Maybe I can find out where the cantor is.'

Brother Nicholas shook his head, unsure of the plan. 'But you'll get into trouble . . .'

'Trouble?' Will hooted in disgust. 'You mean like de Flexburgh and his toadies? What trouble did they get into for all that crap they brought down on us? Eh? Nothing at all, that's what. The prior ordered them to say a few Hail Marys and that was about it. They should have been flogged and kicked out for their part in this!'

Neither Will nor Nicholas had spoken to any of de Flexburgh's friends, but rumours had spread since the attack, and it was now common knowledge that the wayward monks had been inebriated in Selby, publicly fondling the girls they were in relationships with, and throwing money around as if they were wealthy young noblemen.

Which some of them were, of course, but first and foremost they were supposed to be monks with no worldly possessions, never mind purses bulging with coins.

Their extravagant, arrogant behaviour had enraged the people of Selby that day, particularly the lower classes with barely a penny to their name, and the riotous mob had been the result.

So went the rumour, but Will knew there must be more to it.

Who were the soldiers who had been on the periphery of the undisciplined rabble? What was their part in this? Had they taken the cantor? Why?

'Trouble,' Will repeated in disgust, and he strode off, Nicholas at his back.

A short time later the powerfully built ex-mercenary was out of his black robe and dressed in a worn, dirty white tunic, faded green breeches and a much-mended brown cloak – clothes the monks took in as charity and handed out to the needy.

Well, Will was needy – in need of a disguise so the people of Selby wouldn't recognise him as a monk and run him out of town.

He found an old hatchet used for chopping wood out in the garden, and hammered the blade against the wall until it fell off, leaving him with a fine little cudgel that he could carry, hidden, inside his cloak. He'd not meet the people of Selby again without some means of defending himself.

'How will you get out the gates without anyone seeing you?' Nicholas asked as he watched Will crafting his makeshift yet deadly weapon. He looked up at the sky, gesturing at the bright sun. It would be hard, if not impossible, to sneak out on such a fine day.

'Like this,' Will replied, and he walked straight up to the gates, not caring who saw him, lifted the big wooden bar off and tossed it on the ground. 'Lock them behind me, Brother – I'll be back in a few hours, so listen out for my knock!'

He winked and slipped out, patting the cudgel in his belt reassuringly.

Selby was a small town – someone would have the information he needed . . .

* * *

Selby might well have been a small town, but it took a single man much longer to cover it on foot than Will had expected. His plan was to wander around the town centre, buying odds and ends from the stalls there, and visiting some of the local alehouses in the hope he'd overhear some drunk with a loose tongue mention the attack on the abbey. He would miss afternoon prayers of course, but no one would care, even if they noticed.

It had seemed a great plan when he'd walked there with hopes of finding the cantor's whereabouts within an hour or two, but by early afternoon he realised the futility of it.

He'd bought fish from the fishmonger, even though he could have caught the brown trout himself in the Ouse easily enough; he'd spent a coin on a meat pie from a fat baker, who must have saved the best cuts of meat for his own table as the savoury treat was gristly and filled with salt and spices to disguise its lack of flavour; and he'd drunk warm ale in four taverns without hearing a single word about the cantor or even the assault on Selby Abbey.

In short, his day had been a tedious waste of time and he wished more than ever that Robin Hood was still around to guide him. Will had never been a true leader – he'd always worked better as a second-in-command, following the orders of others. And doling out violence, of course – he'd always been an expert at that.

He wandered into yet another alehouse, this one on the western outskirts of town, bearing a weather-beaten sign that named it as Osgood's Rest, and he wondered idly who the hell Osgood might have been.

His heart sank when he noticed the dingy establishment had only one other customer. He wasn't likely to overhear much gossip in such a quiet place, but the thought of moving on and repeating the process at another alehouse was too exasperating, so Will bought a drink and sat on a rickety stool by the window.

A cool breeze came in through the unglazed opening, masking the smell of stale beer and vomit, and the ale was surprisingly fresh compared to the piss-water he'd been sold in the previous taverns. He wished he could just pay for a room, put his feet up for the day, and get roaring drunk before stumbling off to bed.

Swallowing a long pull of the drink, he sighed in pleasure and wiped his lips, shaking his head and dismissing the thought of staying out all night. He should be back at the abbey for Vespers . Again, he doubted anyone would miss him, but if he allowed himself to slip back into his old ways there would be no point in life as a monk.

'Bless me, Father, for I have sinned,' he muttered wryly, tipping the contents of the mug into his mouth again. 'But this is some damn fine ale.'

As he sat there, a happy glow spreading throughout his body, he stared out of the window, the occasional conversation between the landlord and the other customer nothing more than a formless hum in the background as he watched a scrawny dog relieve itself against the wall of the adjacent building before wandering off.

Osgood's Rest was situated on a quiet street which didn't see much human traffic, at this time of day at least. Perhaps it came alive after sundown, Will mused, when the whores and other night-dwellers appeared.

There was a stirring in his loins at the thought of wanton women – it had been many, many months since he'd last enjoyed the pleasures of the flesh – and he tried to think of other things. That bastard Brother de Flexburgh, for example.

The line of thought was no good though, as Will knew the tall monk availed himself of the services of prostitutes as well as enjoying a close relationship with at least one woman within this town.

Jealousy swamped Scaflock.

I'd better say ten Hail Marys to atone for all these wicked thoughts when I get back to the abbey, he mused, staring out of the open window blearily; then his eyes widened and he leaned forward, the old stool creaking in distress as Will watched the man that was striding past the alehouse.

It was the butcher he'd seen with the mob yesterday – the one with the black beard, bloodstained apron and, more significantly, the man who'd been closest to the grim-looking soldiers Will had marked out as the most curious of all the attackers.

Hurriedly, he tossed the remainder of the ale into his mouth – it was too good to leave behind, after all – and dashed out into the street, where he saw the broad shoulders of the butcher disappearing into the distance.

At last, he'd found someone that might be able to help him find the cantor.

* * *

Will jogged after the butcher but his quarry had turned onto one of the narrow side-streets and it seemed hopeless. There was no sign of the man, and Scaflock was lost again.

'Damn it, I might as well just head back to the abbey.' His head was spinning slightly from the effects of the ale he'd consumed that afternoon, and the anger that was building inside him wasn't helping matters.

He'd wasted the day looking for a clue – any clue, no matter how small – to the cantor's fate, only to let the one opportunity he'd found slip through his fingers.

Wandering along a street that he hoped would eventually turn back east and lead him home to Selby Abbey, he failed to take notice of the shop on the corner. He walked another dozen paces before his ale-addled mind made sense of what he'd seen in his peripheral vision, and with a slowly spreading grin, he spun to make sure.

It was a butcher's shop.

Leaning his head back and staring up at the sky between the buildings that flanked the street, he sucked in a deep, calming breath but gagged on the heavy stench of raw meat filling the air. Telling himself to get a grip, he strode purposefully back towards the shop.

'Come on, God, let this be the man I'm looking for,' he prayed softly as he walked in through the door, eyeing the meat pies and the joints of salted meat that hung within the large premises.

'Can I help you?' A burly man appeared from another door at the rear of the building, the stained apron marking him as the owner of the place, and Will eyed him in relief.

It was indeed the man that had been with the mob attacking the abbey.

Will wasn't particularly charismatic, and he certainly had no silver tongue with which he could charm information out of people. He'd also never been one to throw money away on a bribe. His old captains Robin Hood and Adam Bell would likely have made friends with the butcher, impressed him with their magnetism, and drawn out what they wanted to know easily enough within a few minutes.

That wasn't Will's way.

'You were at Selby Abbey the other day,' he growled, covering the distance between himself and the butcher in a heartbeat, grasping the bearded man by the throat and lifting him up off his feet. 'Weren't you?'

He punctuated the question by slamming the butcher's back against the wall. When the man struggled, Will increased the pressure on his windpipe and kneed him between the legs for good measure.

'I know you were there, you arsehole, because I saw you with my own eyes. So don't try to deny it – I'm a man of God and it's a sin to lie to a monk.'

The butcher's eyes were wide with fear and fast-approaching asphyxiation, but he somehow managed to draw his brows together in disbelief. Could this red-faced lunatic truly be one of the Benedictines?

'Aye, I'm a monk,' Will hissed, seeing the man's confusion. 'Why do you think I have this stupid tonsure?'

'What . . . what do you want?'

'Information.' Will released the pressure on the butcher's neck slightly, just enough to let the man breathe and answer his questions. 'That's all. Once you've told me what you know, you can be about your business and I'll be on my way.'

The butcher stared at him from bulging eyes for a moment, defeated, but then the red-rimmed blue orbs flickered slightly to a point behind Will and, at the same time, there was an almost imperceptible creak as a floorboard was depressed.

Instinctively, Will dropped the butcher onto the ground and whirled away, just as a meat cleaver sliced the air where his shoulder had been.

Spinning, the monk saw a skinny lad of about fifteen years clumsily drawing his arm back for another swing with the great rectangular blade, and Will exploded forward, his powerful legs launching him at the attacker. Pulling his cudgel from his belt as he moved, he swung it in a shallow arc so it connected with the boy's cheekbone. As the lad fell backwards, Will followed through with a thundering left hook that smashed his opponent onto the floor.

'That's my son, you bastard,' the supine butcher wheezed, hatred and fury burning like hellfire in his eyes. 'My son!'

Will calmly turned, and strode back to stand gazing down at the man on the brown-stained floor. 'You should have thought of the consequences to your family before you and your friends attacked a house of God, shouldn't you?'

'I'll kill you for this, you—'

Will fell, dropping his knee onto the prostrate butcher's chest, ending the man's diatribe in a blast of agonised air.

'You'll do nothing. Nothing! Do you still not know who I am?'

The butcher stared up, gasping for breath, but at last there was a flicker of recognition in his eyes, followed soon after by the blood draining from his face.

'Will Scarlet? I heard you'd joined the monks but I didn't believe it was really true . . .'

'It's true. Now enough of this damn nonsense! If you'd just given me the information I wanted at the start, you and your boy would still be standing.'

The butcher sucked in a deep, resigned breath, eyeing his fallen son to make sure the lad was breathing, and then he nodded.

'All right. What do you want to know?'

* * *

Will headed back to Selby Abbey, his mind in a whirl as he contemplated the information the butcher had given him.

It didn't make much sense, and again Will wished he had someone to guide him. Someone wise and cunning like Robin, or even the likeable giant, Little John.

But he was on his own now, and he'd need to solve this problem himself. The responsibility weighed heavily on his shoulders.

As he walked through the streets in the late-afternoon sun, sellers still hawked their wares and a child looked up at him hopefully, cap in grubby hand. Will dropped a coin into the sad receptacle without any conscious thought as he remembered his conversation with the butcher.

'What made you come to the abbey?' he'd demanded of the man. 'What happened to rile you and your fellow villagers so much that particular day?'

Of course, it had been Brother de Flexburgh and his useless friends who'd been the cause of the upset, but what had actually precipitated the mob's anger, the butcher couldn't say.

'So how did you end up chasing after them?' Will had wanted to know. 'Did you hear a commotion in the street? What was it?'

'Shouts.' The butcher had nodded. 'In the street, aye, you're right. They were so loud that I came out to see what the hell was happening. There was a couple of men hurrying past, complaining about those damn monks being drunk – again – and starting a fight. Again!'

Will had seen the righteous fury building in the butcher's eyes and he understood it completely. Here was a man up to his elbows, literally, in blood every day, trying to provide a life for his family. Meanwhile, de Flexburgh swanned around the place with his idle mates, drinking and whoring with their noses in the air, never working a day in their lives as they wasted their rich families' fortunes and enjoyed the comforts – such as they were – of the abbey.

'One of those so-called monks had his way with the daughter of my neighbour, so I was glad to lock up my shop and follow the men.'

'Who were they? Did you know them?'

The butcher had seemed taken aback by the question and shook his head at last. 'No, never seen them before. Hadn't thought of it at the time, I was too caught up in what was going on.'

Will sighed. In such a small place as Selby you'd assume any stranger would be remarked upon instantly, but it seemed the depth of hatred against the monks overcame even the insular nature of a man like this butcher.

'All right, so you joined the mob these men were gathering and ended up at the abbey.'

'I never took nothing,' the butcher broke in vehemently. 'When the fighting started I buggered off back here.'

Will felt sure the man was lying – he'd seen the butcher land more than one kick on the murdered Brother de la Breuer, but that didn't interest him.

'What happened with those men that started the whole thing? Where did they go?'

'How would I know? I told you, I—'

Will had leaned in and grabbed the butcher by the throat again, squeezing brutally as he hauled the man back to his feet with apparently little effort. 'Don't lie to me, you fat turd. I know you were there in the abbey and I know you were part of the group that beat the monk to death. So, unless you want me to tell the law what I know, you'll answer my questions.'

'Tell him, Da.' The butcher's son had come to with a groan and pleaded then in a harsh voice, too frightened of this violent ex-outlaw to renew his earlier attempted assault. 'Just tell him what he wants to know.'

'Aye, go on.' Will glared at the butcher, who relented, trying to nod against the pressure on his neck.

'Fine! Yes, I was in the abbey.' He bent to gather his breath, using a hand to steady himself against the meat-flecked chopping table. 'I never stole nothing though, I swear it.'

'I don't care if you stole the damn Holy Grail,' Will interjected. 'I just want to know what the strangers did when they left Selby.'

The butcher stood gasping and wheezing for long moments as Will glared impatiently, before, at last, he spoke again.

'They didn't steal anything either. Not that I saw anyway, although I wasn't taking much notice to be honest. They didn't even come inside the building, just headed for one of the older Benedictines, roughed him up a bit, then dragged him away out the gates. Lord knows what they did with him.' The gears turned slowly in his head before he finally realised he might be implicated in another murder. 'Is the old monk all right? Never thought much about it until now. I assumed you lot knew those men that took him off.'

'Why would you assume that?'

'Well, I saw them talking to one of your brothers in the market, a couple of hours before we started chasing after 'em.'

Will had straightened at that piece of vital information. 'Who were they talking to? Describe him.'

'I don't need to describe him – I know who he is well enough. De Flexburgh's his name. He's the one that defiled my neighbour's daughter, dirty bastard that he is.

Man of God? Pah. Just as well he's a fast runner or the people would have done for him instead of that other one, aye, and I'd have stamped on his smug face myself, I'm not ashamed to admit it!'

Will contemplated all this as the great stone walls of Selby Abbey came into sight, wondering what he should do next. What would Robin Hood do?

His first thought was to find de Flexburgh and beat a confession from the man, but he suspected that would be the wrong move. The tall monk would surely have his henchmen around him, and even if Will were to incapacitate some of them, the alarm would be raised and Will would be stopped before his righteous violence could extract the needed information.

Assuming the idler knew anything of course. Perhaps the hard-looking strangers had simply been threatening de Flexburgh before the mob unleashed its fury. There might be a perfectly innocent reason for the conversation the butcher claimed he'd witnessed.

If only he could get the tall monk alone, one-on-one . . .

It was growing late now, and the sun began to dip beneath the high walls which had failed so miserably to provide the abbey with any meaningful defence. Will decided to simply head for his pallet in the dormitory to think on what he'd learned.

Maybe he'd even pray to God for guidance.

* * *

White light streamed in through the small window above Will's bed in the dormitory, and he woke up, shielding his eyes with a muscular forearm.

The light was blinding, and fearfully, knowing its radiance could come from no earthly source, he wondered whether to grab the axe-handle he'd left on the floor with his clothes, or drop to his knees and pray again, as he had before retiring.

A voice came to him – not to his ears; it seemed to speak directly into his head – and he held his breath, concentrating intently, trying to make out the words which came in a rush, but he despaired.

It was impossible!

The sense of missing out on some great, world-shattering moment consumed him and he opened his mouth to cry out in rage.

The shout seemed to catch in his throat, and Will realised at last that he was sitting up in his bed, the dormitory pitch-black and the gentle snores of his dozing brothers all around him.

He'd been dreaming.

The sense of despair didn't leave him though. On the contrary, it seemed to crowd in even closer now that he knew the whole thing had been a meaningless trick of his own mind, and he lay back with a strangled gasp.

He tried to remember the words he'd heard in the dream – to catch the waking edge of it – but it had slipped away and, for some bizarre reason, all he wanted to do was fill his belly with meat and cheese. He was as hungry as he could ever remember being in his entire life, so despite the fact that it was the middle of the night, he stood and fumbled on the floor for his robe, not caring if he woke the rest of the sleeping monks.

His grasping fingers found it at last and he draped it around his sweating body. Silently, he opened the door to the chamber and made his way along the corridor by touch and memory, heading for the kitchen, still trying to regain the dream.

It wasn't far to the kitchen but, having never tried to reach it in the pitch-black before, it took Will longer than he expected to get there, and the sense of hunger seemed to grow with every step until, at last, he pushed open the adjoining door from the refectory and stopped dead in his tracks.

To his dark-accustomed eyes the dim light of a candle seemed as blinding as the God-light in his dream, and he shrank back into the shadows, realising someone else had shared his night-time hunger.

For a moment Will stood, thinking, but his stomach rumbled angrily and he threw caution aside. The abbot had been insensible since the attack and the monks had much more to worry about than a brother stealing a crust in the night.

Taking a deep breath, he straightened his back and strode into the kitchen as if he had every right to be there.

Brother de Flexburgh spun and stared back at him in shock.

'Truly,' Will muttered, a smile twitching the edges of his mouth as he sized up the situation in an instant, 'this is a gift from God Himself.'

Before the taller monk could react, Will lunged forward and punched him hard in the face, then, as de Flexburgh rocked backwards, he followed it up by grabbing his opponent and hammering a knee into his guts, blasting the wind from his lungs and silencing any possible cry of alarm.

To his credit, de Flexburgh did attempt to fight back, but dazed and winded as he was, he had no chance against the one-time killing machine that was Will Scarlet, and before the fight had even begun it was over, the arrogant monk lying on his back on the hard stone floor.

'What are you doing in here in the middle of the night?'

De Flexburgh glared up at Will but there was fear in his eyes as clear as day. They were all alone here.

'I was hungry,' the downed man muttered. 'Had a nightmare, and it left me wanting some meat and cheese.'

Will's brow lowered, wondering how de Flexburgh knew about his own dream. Then, realising it was impossible, he grinned.

God had brought them together, here, for a purpose.

He smiled nastily. 'I'm hungry myself, so we'll share a meal together, eh? Or at least I'll eat and you can watch. But first, you're going to tell me what you know about the cantor's disappearance.'

* * *

It was the old story. Of course it was the old story.

Money.

Will should have known, even without any inkling of the cantor's background.

Apparently Brother de Loup came from a wealthy family. He'd been the second son though, and as a result had been sent away into a life with the Benedictines by his father, while the firstborn had gone on to a glorious life as a knight.

Everyone in Selby Abbey knew this apparently, aside from Will because he had not been there very long.

Brother de Flexburgh certainly knew about it and, owing rather a lot of money in gambling debts to some unsavoury people, had come up with a plan to solve his problems.

'They won't hurt him, I swear. They're just holding him in the forest until the ransom's been paid.'

'What ransom?' Will demanded. 'They haven't even sent a demand as far as I know.'

De Flexburgh flinched at the venomous tone in Will's reply. 'They have! It's just not been read yet since it was sent to the abbot and he's still unconscious. As soon as he wakes up, he'll relay it to the cantor's family, the money will be paid over, and de Loup will be freed.'

'Assuming the family pay your ransom.' Scaflock spat in disgust. 'I came here to get away from filth like you. You make me sick to the very pit of my soul.'

The insult washed over de Flexburgh with no effect, and Will's stomach growled again, reminding him of the hunger his dream had brought on.

He got to his feet, never taking his eyes from his downed opponent, and found some black bread, which he shoved into his mouth and began to chew hungrily.

'Can I get up?'

'No you can't, you bastard,' Will retorted, spitting crumbs in his anger. 'You can lie there like a dog until I'm done! And then we're going to speak to the abbot.'

* * *

Prior Ousthorp was in no mood to allow Will and the sullen Brother de Flexburgh access to the abbot, who, although he'd regained consciousness the previous day, was still understandably weak.

'Whatever you need to see him about, I can deal with it.'

'It's about Brother de Loup,' Will said reluctantly. He still suspected the prior cared little for the abducted cantor, guessing he saw the older man as something of a threat to his position, since de Loup and the abbot had been friends for years.

'What about him?' Ousthorp asked warily.

'A note was sent to Abbot de Wystow, according to . . . this . . .' Will gestured towards the cowed, bloodied de Flexburgh in disgust. 'It's vital the abbot reads, and acts, on the note's instructions, as soon as possible. If he's still unconscious—'

'I'm not,' came a weak shout from inside the chamber, followed by a coughing fit. 'Get me a drink of water, Brother Ousthorp. And let them in.'

The prior glared furiously at the unlikely companions, then pushed the abbot's door open and waved them into the candlelit room, following at their backs and hurrying across to de Wystow's bedside, where he lifted a jug of water and filled a small cup with it.

He handed it to the abbot as Will and de Flexburgh stood, heads bowed respectfully until the old man had slaked his thirst and returned the cup with a shaky sigh.

'Now, what's all this about the cantor?'

'You know he was taken by the rioters, Father?' Will asked.

'Yes. Brother Ousthorp apprised me of the situation when I returned to the land of the living yesterday.' He shook his head and stared balefully at de Flexburgh. 'This is all your fault. Again. What are we going to do with you, boy?'

The tall monk's eyes flared at the abbot's use of the diminutive but he held his peace. De Wystow might let him get away with his disrespectful behaviour but he obviously feared Will's meaty fists would not be so forgiving.

'If the cantor is harmed, it will go badly for you, Brother de Flexburgh, I promise you that in God's name.' The abbot turned to the prior. 'Do we know who took him, or why? What's this note Brother Scaflock mentioned? I know nothing of any note.'

'No, Father,' Ousthorp shook his head. 'We don't know who's behind it, but a note did come yesterday, delivered by a boy from the village. He handed it to one of the monks in the garden, then ran off before I could question him.'

'We do know who's behind it,' Will said, drawing another angry glare from the prior, who didn't seem to appreciate the former wolf's head taking control of the situation.

The abbot looked at Scaflock from beneath lowered brows, ignoring Ousthorp. 'We do?'

'Aye, Father, we do,' Will said. 'It was a group of outlaws—'

'That much is obvious,' the prior groused, but the abbot silenced him with an irritable flick of his hand.

'A group of outlaws,' Will repeated, 'working with this piece of filth here.' He slapped de Flexburgh on the back of the head and the taller monk glared at him in fury, but the beating he'd suffered in the kitchen was fresh in his mind and he held himself in check.

'Here is the note,' the prior muttered, looking unhappily at Will but unable to bring himself to upbraid the new monk for his violence. De Flexburgh deserved it, and more.

Abbot de Wystow took the scrap of parchment that had been folded and sealed with a blob of candle wax, although it bore no seal which was hardly surprising. The abbot inspected the wax and eyed the prior suspiciously –

it wouldn't be the first time Ousthorp had sneaked a look at his private correspondence. The seal appeared intact but it was impossible to tell if it was the original or not, so de Wystow opened out the parchment and squinted at it.

His eyesight was poor nowadays and it took him a few moments to read the short message. Will's heart sank when the abbot groaned and handed the letter back to the prior, who read it for himself.

'What does it say?' Will demanded. 'What's wrong? De Flexburgh told me it was just a ransom note.'

The abbot nodded, ignoring Will's lack of etiquette as he heard the concern in the ex-mercenary's voice.

'So it is.'

'What's the problem then? Pass it on to the cantor's family and they'll pay, right? The outlaws only want money and, from what I hear, Brother de Loup's family has plenty of it.'

He looked at de Flexburgh, who leaned back, out of range of Will's fists, and nodded agreement. 'Yes, that's right. The outlaws won't hurt him, they just want the ransom. I swear it!'

'You swear it?' the abbot demanded, dragging himself upright in the bed. 'What part do you play in this abduction, Brother?'

'I . . . that is, I have some . . .'

Will broke in as de Flexburgh stuttered. 'He has gambling debts which were going to get him into serious trouble, so he set up the cantor's abduction with a group of outlaws he met in an alehouse in Selby. The riot that left you insensible and our abbey smashed up was no accident – Brother de Flexburgh here orchestrated the whole thing.'

'What?' the prior exploded, incandescent with rage. He crossed the room in an instant and grabbed de Flexburgh by the front of his black robe, glaring up at the sullen man. 'Is this true, you great oaf?'

De Flexburgh turned his face away to stare at the wall but the prior shook him roughly. 'Speak, Judas! Is Brother Scaflock's charge correct?'

'Let him go, John,' the abbot sighed. 'You can see from his guilty expression it's true. We'll deal with him, and any other accomplices within our walls, later. For now, we must address the problem of the ransom note.'

'Where does the cantor's family live?' Will asked. 'I'll take word to them, make sure the ransom money is delivered to the outlaws and bring him home safely. You can trust me,' he said, drawing himself up and clenching his fists. 'You know my past. I'll see it done.'

'Ah, Brother Scaflock.' The abbot smiled sadly and shook his head. 'If only it were that simple. You see, the problem is, the cantor's family are as good as penniless.'

There was a stunned silence in the room for a long moment, as the revelation was absorbed.

'No they're not,' de Flexburgh finally said at last, his voice thin, the expression on his face one of disbelief. 'Everyone knows they're amongst the wealthiest families in all England. The ransom the outlaws have asked for is just a drop in the ocean to de Loup's father.'

Even the prior nodded his head and, looking down at the note in his hand, said, 'I must agree, Father Abbot. Seventy pounds? It's a huge sum, but surely just a fraction of the cantor's family wealth.'

'No, you're wrong,' Abbot de Wystow snapped, wagging a finger imperiously at de Flexburgh. 'The de Loups were one of the wealthiest families in England. Were! When the old king was on the throne. But the new king's mother, Isabella, and the co-regent, Mortimer, have no love for the de Loups, who were staunch supporters of the previous regime. They seized much of the family's lands and holdings and, on top of that, the cantor's father suffered catastrophic losses when many of his trading ships were taken by pirates.'

'What are you saying?' de Flexburgh whispered.

'I'm saying there will be no ransom money paid for the cantor's release,' de Wystow raged, slamming his emaciated fists onto the bed. 'What will your outlaw friends do when they find that out?'

The tall monk looked in turn from the abbot to the prior and finally, fearfully, to Will. He didn't say a word, but the expression on his face said enough.

Brother de Loup was as good as dead.

* * *

Abbot de Wystow had a stronger constitution than Will had ever expected, and the old man was back on his feet that same afternoon. He'd agreed with Will's suggestion that Brother de Flexburgh be locked away, at least until the situation with the cantor was resolved. They couldn't run the risk of the wayward monk sneaking off and warning the outlaws that their ransom plans were unexpectedly dead in the water.

His closest friends, Brothers de Whitgift, de Hirst and de Pontefracto were all confined to the dormitory, although Will didn't really see any of those monks as much of a danger. They were drunkards who ignored their vows of chastity to sleep with any woman willing, but they weren't desperate men like de Flexburgh, who seemed to think the world owed him something.

The fire was lit within the abbot's chambers despite the summer heat, and Will wiped his tonsured head with a black sleeve that was already damp with perspiration. After their talk that morning, de Wystow had sent Will to refresh and rest himself, then called the former mercenary back to discuss how best they might help the abducted cantor.

'It's fortuitous that God sent you to us at this time, Brother Scaflock,' the abbot said thoughtfully as he stared into the flames in the hearth. 'We have some hardy men here in the abbey, but none with your experience of situations like this.'

'What he means is: you're a wolf's head yourself so you'll know how these scum think better than anyone.'

Will's eyes narrowed at the prior's insulting tone. 'You're right, Brother Ousthorp. I *was* an outlaw, and I slapped more than one clergyman about for talking down to me.'

The prior flinched as Scaflock jerked his head forward threateningly, and the abbot demanded both men be silent. A small, approving smile tugged at one corner of his thin lips though, as he turned back to Will.

'What should we do, in your opinion?'

Will had been thinking about the problem all day and there seemed to be no simple solution. 'We need to know where the outlaws are holding the cantor hostage. If we knew the location of their camp we – or at least the bailiff's men, if he ever arrives – could surround them, and hopefully make them let our brother go without harming him.'

'Do you think they will? Harm him, I mean.'

The abbot looked worried but Will couldn't lie to him. 'Aye, if they don't get what they want, they'll slit his throat and move on to their next camp miles away. We'd never find them then. I have no doubt about it.'

'Surely we have some time though,' the prior demanded. 'They want their ransom money, and it would take at least a week for it to get here, if the cantor's father actually had it. They won't harm him until then surely, that would be ridiculous.'

Will shrugged. He'd seen men – and not just outlaws – do plenty of ridiculous, vicious things in his time. 'They won't kill him for at least a few days,' he conceded. 'Probably.'

'What are we going to do then?' the abbot muttered, grimacing at a twinge of pain before lowering himself slowly into a deeply cushioned chair.

'I assume the note they sent has a location where they want the ransom money left?'

De Wystow nodded at Will's query and pulled the folded parchment from the pouch on his belt, then stared at it. 'A tree stump painted red not far from a bridge near Wistow, beside a great oak. There are directions here. Apparently they'll be watching for our messenger and there's warnings against bringing lawmen or guards along. They've obviously planned this quite thoroughly.'

'So, we send someone with some of the ransom and ask the outlaws for more time to gather the rest.'

'Where are we going to find a sum like that?' the prior demanded irritably. 'This is an abbey, not a palace.'

'There's gold crosses and other priceless altar goods all over this building. Including around your neck,' Will spat, angered that this man would put trinkets before the life of the cantor. 'He looked across at the abbot, whose face paled at the idea of losing his abbey's wealth, but to his credit, de Wystow nodded.

'If it buys Brother de Loup a few more days for the bailiff to come and bring these sinners to justice, it will be worth it.'

'That's it?' the prior demanded. 'That's your plan?'

Will smiled, although the expression held little humour.

'Not entirely. I'll be behind the monk that delivers our ransom. I'll track the outlaws to their camp and return here. Then, when the bailiff does finally get to the abbey, I'll be able to lead him straight there.'

Ousthorp was somewhat mollified by that, although he still glared suspiciously at Will, as though he thought the former outlaw might run off and join up with the cantor's abductors once they had the abbey's wealth in their hands. Wisely, the prior held his peace.

'Who will we send to them?' the abbot mused, getting to his feet and pacing slowly up and down the cosy chamber. 'This could very well mean death for whoever goes.'

'I'll ask for volunteers,' the prior said, and with a final suspicious look at Will, he swept from the room.

The abbot stood up with some effort and filled two cups from a flagon of wine on a table next to the window. He handed one to Will, who took it gladly and drank with pleasure, realising this was no cheap stuff.

'The prior is a good man, really.'

Will raised an eyebrow in mock disbelief and the abbot smiled, sipping his own wine.

'I think he feels he has to be some severe disciplinarian to offset the fact so many of the brothers see me as a soft touch. But deep down, Ousthorp is a decent fellow and, more importantly to me since I'd have trouble recalling what I ate for breakfast this morning, an excellent administrator.'

They stood in companionable silence for a while, hearing the prior's loud voice moving here and there around the abbey grounds as he sought a volunteer to carry the ransom to the outlaws.

'What will you do if you're discovered tracking those men?'

Will shrugged. 'I've got a nice sturdy club and I can look after myself, have no fears on that count.'

'You'd better get down to the kitchen then, Brother,' the abbot eventually said, tossing back the last of his wine and arching his shoulders in a shiver, as if it was cold in the sweltering, fire-lit, room. 'You'll need provisions for your journey tomorrow morning. I know Wistow isn't far, but who knows where the wolf's heads are hiding? Tell the bottler to give you whatever you ask for or he'll answer to me.'

Will returned the old man's smile and, dismissed, headed out along the corridor to réquisition his supplies for the hunt.

* * *

The volunteer Prior Ousthorp had found was none other than Will's young friend, Brother Nicholas de Houghton. More than one of the monks had put their names forward for the task, such was the cantor's popularity in the abbey, but Nicholas, despite his limp, was the youngest of the bunch and seemed best suited to the job of delivering the ransom. He couldn't run properly, but he was fit and able to walk for hours.

It was a sensible choice but Will prayed the lad wouldn't find himself on the wrong side of the outlaws.

'Are you sure you want to do this? If the wolf's head that comes to collect the ransom is drunk or just in a bad mood you could find yourself murdered.'

It was early morning and a fine, damp mist covered the gardens around the abbey as Will and Nicholas prepared to leave, Abbot de Wystow and the prior at their backs having given them final, unneeded advice on how to complete their tasks.

Nicholas nodded emphatically. 'I'm ready. I like the cantor just as much as you and I want to see him back here safely.'

'Good man.' Will smiled, clapping the younger monk on the arm.

'Take care not to lose that sack,' the prior growled, fixing a steely glare on Nicholas. 'Half the abbey's treasures are in there. We don't want some other, different gang of thieves stealing it. Make sure it's well spent.'

'He's got a point,' Will said. 'You could do with a weapon in case some opportunist robbers attack you. Have you got anything?'

'No,' Nicholas admitted. 'I learned to shoot a hunting bow when I was growing up, but I don't have one. Or anything else. Is it really necessary? If some outlaws want me dead I doubt I'd be able to stop them even if I was carrying Excalibur.' He patted his leg ruefully. 'I can't move very fast, remember?'

Before Will could reply Abbot de Wystow walked slowly forward and Will noticed a bundle in his arms.

'Nicholas may not want a weapon but you should have a decent one, Brother Scaflock. Here.' He stretched out his scrawny old arms and Will, surprised, unwrapped the cloth that covered the abbot's bundle. As he did so, a boyish grin spread over his face.

'My old sword.'

'Indeed,' de Wystow confirmed. 'In most circumstances when someone comes to join us, we sell their unwanted possessions but . . .' He shrugged. 'I kept this – thought you might need it again one day. Just as well I did, eh?'

Will looked at the sword with its plain, unadorned scabbard, but didn't take it from the abbot's outstretched hands.

He'd given up this weapon freely when he took up the life of a Benedictine monk. His previous life of violence and sin was behind him.

The abbot saw the conflict in Will's eyes.

'Take it,' he commanded. 'God has a purpose for us all, and your purpose is to bring our friend Brother de Loup back from the clutches of evil. If that means you using this sword once again, well . . . our Lord goes with you, my son.'

'Amen,' the prior grunted, and Will was pleased to see grudging respect in the man's eyes.

He was to be an instrument of God.

So be it.

He took his old sword from the abbot, whose arms were visibly shaking from the effort of holding the weapon, and threaded his belt through the scabbard so it hung by his left hip, just as it had done for more than twenty years before he'd joined the abbey.

The abbot smiled at the sight of the former wolf's head, who somehow seemed whole again, as if he'd been an incomplete man without the deadly blade at his side.

'Here . . .' Will grinned, reaching inside his robe to pull out the club he'd made, before handing it to Brother Nicholas. 'Take it. Hide it the same way I did. Here – let me show you . . .'

Moments later the crude but potentially deadly wooden weapon was secreted inside Brother Nicholas's clothes and that was it – they were ready to deliver the ransom.

'Please,' Abbot de Wystow said earnestly as they began to walk towards the gate. 'Take care of yourselves. The cantor is an old, close friend of mine but . . . you're good men.' His expression was one of sadness now, at the injustice and darkness in the world. 'I wouldn't want to lose either of you to those vicious criminals.'

The prior didn't manage a smile but he nodded silent encouragement and made the sign of the cross as the two messengers of God walked through the damaged gates to carry out their mission.

Will took one last, lingering look at the great stone building as they joined the main road and headed north-west towards Wistow. The rising sun broke through the clouds at that moment, framing the abbey, wreathed in mist as it was, in a beautiful golden halo.

It almost seemed like an omen, although whether it was good or bad, only time would tell . . .

* * *

The road to Wistow was a well-maintained one, allowing the travellers to make good time. They feared the outlaws might have sent spies to watch the abbey, so, when they reached Selby, Will waved an exaggerated farewell to Nicholas and headed off into the town to buy a meat pasty. The younger man continued on towards Wistow, his limping gait worrying Scaflock since it might mark Nicholas as an even easier target than he already was.

Will hung around in Selby for a short time, allowing a gap to open between them as he ate his pasty and ignored the dirty looks from the townsfolk. Eventually he hurried back to the main road, which he planned to flank at a safe distance until they reached the ransom drop-off point.

He was breathing heavily by the time he finally spotted his friend in the near distance, his limp plain even to Will who had never had the best eyesight, and he blew a small sigh of relief that the monk hadn't been waylaid while out of his view.

When discussing the plan with the abbot, it had been suggested Will go on an hour ahead of Nicholas, then, once nearer the drop-off place, conceal himself, but Scaflock had rejected the idea. There were numerous other outlaws living in the greenwood, and any of them might stumble upon Nicholas. Without the ransom goods he carried, this whole scheme would be ruined and the cantor as good as dead. No – the limping monk needed a guard of some sort and it had to be someone out of sight yet close enough to help should Nicholas be waylaid.

'We'll pray for your success,' the abbot had promised, and Will had been grateful. He would take any help he could get.

The prayers earnestly rising up from Selby Abbey seemed to do their job, as Nicholas had only passed half a dozen other parties on the road, all of them innocent traders or similar, before the smoke that marked the location of a small village – Wistow – appeared on the horizon. Will could even make out the little bridge that crossed the shallow water of Black Fen Drain.

The River Ouse was somewhere to the east, although too far away to see, and now Nicholas stopped, looking in that direction, head swivelling left and right as his eyes searched for the great old oak the outlaws' ransom note had mentioned. At last he spotted it and moved off in its direction as Will nodded in appreciation. The lad must have been nervous, frightened of attack by the cantor's abductors now they were so close to the drop-off area, and yet Nicholas hadn't glanced back even once to where he knew his protector must be concealed.

Instead, the young monk moved as fast as his crooked limb would allow, over the uneven, often marshy terrain, directly towards the solitary, venerable oak that must have stood guard over these fields for hundreds of years, as Will came along behind, using juniper bushes and bracken as cover.

Eventually, Scaflock knew he could follow no further. The outlaws would certainly have at least one lookout nearby, watching the drop-off location. He would simply need to pray that Nicholas would deliver the ransom and head back to the abbey safely.

The sun was high overhead as it neared midday, and Will settled down to wait, hidden amongst a small grove of birch trees that was fringed by masses of summer foliage. He was used to waiting like this, for something to happen. He'd done it many times in his life, as a mercenary and as an outlaw, and he was able to control his anxiety better than most men would in such a situation.

He undid the laces on the sack the bottler had prepared for him back at the abbey, and peered inside. Minutes later he'd shelled and eaten two hard-boiled eggs, some cheese and a few strawberries, washing the lot down with sips from a water skin.

It was hot even within the shade of the trees, and he would have liked nothing better than to lie down and sleep, but Will Scaflock was far too experienced to fall into that trap and he stared out through a gap in the foliage, hopefully awaiting the reappearance of Brother Nicholas.

How long would a ransom drop-off take? Will had finished his lunch and he felt like the sun had covered much of the sky before, at last, thanks be to God, Brother Nicholas reappeared, minus the sack which had held the abbey's coveted valuables.

It was done, then. The fact the young monk still lived suggested the outlaws had accepted their offer of half the ransom now with half to follow later, and that meant Will had a chance to locate the cantor before he was disposed of.

Scaflock watched from his hiding place in the undergrowth as Brother Nicholas limped back towards the main road and then set off back in the direction of Selby, his gait seeming somehow more jaunty than it had been on the way there.

Will's lip curled in a half-smile at the lad's obvious happiness on successfully completing his mission, then he settled back down to wait again, until both Nicholas and the outlaw with the abbey's extorted hoard left the area.

He ate more of the bread and cheese, drank half of the remaining water in the leather skin, then, hoping enough time had passed, rose to a crouch and hurried through the field of near-ripe wheat towards the massive oak.

As he approached it he felt a pang of nostalgia, remembering a similar ancient tree which he and his friends had camped close to in Barnsdale, back when he was a wolf's head himself.

Pushing the gloomy feelings aside, he quickly reached the gnarled old trunk and stood close to it, eyes searching the area for any threats, hand on the pommel of his newly returned sword, ears straining for any sound, which, he hoped, would be obvious out here in the middle of nowhere.

There was nothing other than the gentle buzz of bees harvesting the carpet of nearby myriad flowers and the harsh, angry croaking of a sleek carrion crow that stalked the ground searching for food, a beady eye fixing occasionally, warily, on the watching Scaflock.

Of the abbey's sack of valuables there was no sign. Whoever had collected it from young Nicholas had presumably hastened back to the outlaws' camp without delay.

Relaxing a little, Will moved forward and began to examine the ground. He saw Brother Nicholas's footprints and ignored them, the simple, flat monks' sandals leaving an obvious pattern in the soft mud. Of much more interest were the tracks that clearly met, then moved away from Nicholas's, leaving a trail to the west. Scaflock drew up a mental image of the area, trying to discern where the wolf's head might have been heading. In such an empty landscape, the outlaw would have headed directly – as the crow flies – towards his camp.

The map in Will's head suggested one of two places: Bigging; or, slightly further off, Kirk Fenton.

It was a start.

Unless the outlaw who'd taken the ransom had known he'd be tracked and left a false trail for any pursuers . . .

Will discarded that idea and took a last look around, making sure he hadn't missed anything. Then he began to run in the direction the outlaw's footprints led, hoping they'd not become lost in the fields, and that, ideally, he'd be able to catch sight of the outlaw in the distance and follow him straight to the cantor.

Will felt good. After long months cooped up in Selby Abbey with nothing to do but pray, sing and tidy the place, this was fine. Real man's work.

He grinned as he ran, then frowned at the thought of the kidnapped cantor, but he dropped a hand to the pommel of his sword and the grim smile returned to his face as his palm closed around its familiar leather-bound hilt.

He was going to rescue Brother de Loup or die in the attempt.

* * *

Truly God was on Will's side that day. His quarry's footprints were invisible on the open, summer-dry ground, but every so often the man had passed through a stand of trees or other thick foliage which had retained the previous evening's rain within their shadows. Those damp sections of terrain left clear traces of the outlaw's footprints, making it fairly easy for Scaflock to follow the trail.

The fugitive was faster than Will though, and the trailing monk didn't catch so much as a glimpse of the wolf's head during the entire chase.

It eventually became clear that the tracks were leading further north than Bigging, and Will cursed, knowing the outlaw must be heading for Kirk Fenton. That meant an extra few miles of running he could have done without.

There was no help for it though, and he was glad he'd been able to rest and regain his strength earlier. He wished he was twenty years younger as his calf muscles began to burn from the exertion and his breathing became more laboured as time went on but, at last, he neared the tiny village of Kirk Fenton and stopped to take a look around.

This area had some of the flattest terrain in all England. Nothing but farms and fields for miles, broken only occasionally by trees, almost-dry streams, and narrow dirt tracks that passed for roads.

It was a terrible place for an outlaw gang to hide out.

'There.'

Will focused on a thick grove of birch trees on the horizon, some way to the north of the village, and felt sure he'd located Brother de Loup's kidnappers' camp.

The unmistakeable, greasy smoke from a good-sized cooking fire rose in a column from the centre of that grove, easily visible to anyone within a mile of the place, and the monk's mouth watered as he imagined what succulent roasting beast was sending such alluring plumes of grey up into the summer sky.

'God, I could go for some cooked beef right now,' Will muttered as he stared at the distant campsite. 'With the edges crisp and burnt from the fire . . . A nice piece of freshly baked bread and some cool ale . . .'

He wiped the sweat from his brow with the sleeve of his black robe and looked around. Seeing a solitary Scots pine just a few paces away, he made his way slowly towards it.

'This will have to do for now,' he mumbled, sitting down with his back against the trunk of the tree and emptying the remainder of his food pack onto the ground.

That was surely the outlaws' camp ahead and it gave Will heart, for they were clearly fools with little woodcraft to give away their position with a fire like that. Either that or they were too stupid to think anyone might attack them away out here in the middle of nowhere.

Still, despite all that, he couldn't just run towards the grove of trees, sword drawn, and hope to frighten them off. If the outlaws saw him coming on the open terrain they'd certainly have the sense to organise their defences and he'd have no chance against them. They might even kill the cantor and that was the last thing Will wanted.

No, he would wait until it was dark, then get in close and confirm this was indeed where Brother de Loup was being held, before making his way back to Selby to lead the law here in greater numbers.

For now, he rested against the tree he'd chosen, grasped his sword and allowed himself to fall into a light slumber until night fell.

* * *

'They really are fools,' Will said to himself a few hours later as he made his way carefully across the open ground in the gloom of the moonlit evening.

The outlaws' campfire hadn't been banked with the onset of night – on the contrary it seemed to glow like a great orange beacon in the surrounding darkness, offering Scaflock a target he couldn't fail to see.

Or hear.

The sound of raucous singing carried across the flat ground, the dead, still air doing nothing to dissipate it, and Will fancied he could make out individual voices in the overall rabble.

As he approached the noisy campsite he drew his sword, the blade smeared with mud earlier in the day to dull the shine – he didn't want it glinting in the moon's pale light and giving him away – and peered into the birch trees that fringed the outlaws' camp.

Robin Hood would have had lookouts posted in those trees, vigilant for the approach of any threat, but Will didn't really expect that the cantor's foolhardy, overconfident abductors would follow such precautions. It didn't hurt to be careful though, and he moved slowly, silently, like a shadow, from tree to tree, as he neared the blazing fire, epicentre of probably the merriest celebration the area had ever witnessed.

'What'll you do with your share of the ransom once we melt it all down?' a voice demanded, and Will crouched in the long grass, waiting, listening.

'Buy a whole shitload of ale!' came the answering cry, and there was a chorus of gleeful agreement from at least half a dozen throats.

'Get a few whores too,' another voice grunted, to more cries of delight.

'What if they don't pay us the rest of the money though?'

'Who cares?' someone replied. 'We've got plenty here today already. If that limping fool doesn't come back with the rest we'll just kill the old monk and move on.'

The drunken conversation continued as Scaflock moved forward again, hugging the trees. He might have made his name as a ferocious, uncompromising fighter with a horrendous temper, but, when needed, he could move as silently as one of the Saracen assassins so feared by the Crusaders.

And it was just as well.

To his side, so close he could smell it, came the splattering of liquid striking the earth and Will stopped dead in his tracks.

He peered into the blackness and focused on the figure of a tall man emptying his bladder.

With great reluctance, Will refrained from skewering the easy target. He wasn't there to attack the outlaws – he was only there to confirm the cantor was still alive.

The outlaw finished relieving himself, laced his breeches back up and stumbled back to the fire as Will followed in his wake, still keeping close to the shadows, alert for any more of the drunken fools.

When he could see the faces around the fire he stopped moving and stared, trying to get his eyes adjusted to the orange glare. He didn't recognise any of the men at first, until he noticed a long-haired, bearded fellow who stood a short distance outside the brightest circle of firelight.

He knew that one all right. He'd been at Selby Abbey when it was attacked and the cantor taken.

And then Will's middle-aged eyes had to make another adjustment as he tried to focus on something at the bearded outlaw's feet. He peered into the gloom and, finally, nodded in relief – it was the cantor, and he was still alive, apparently chewing on a cut of meat.

Despite his tasty meal it was obvious Brother de Loup hadn't had an easy time with his kidnappers as he bore a livid purple bruise, and the beaten, broken expression on his usually cheerful face enraged Will to the extent he almost attacked the outlaws there and then. He would be hopelessly outnumbered, even if he did have the element of surprise for a few moments.

He stared at the cantor for a time, trying to make sure the man was, despite the bruising, in good health. It was impossible to tell at this distance and in the poor light, but the monk still lived and that was the important thing.

Now Will just had to sneak safely away from this vipers' nest and return to Selby with the cantor's location so the bailiff could get here. And Will would make damn sure he was a part of the rescue party . . .

'I knew you'd come in close for a good look.'

The familiar voice froze him in his tracks and he turned his head.

Sure enough, leaning against a tree was the tall, burly, unmistakeable silhouette of Brother Robert de Flexburgh.

The man was staring directly at Will.

'You were only supposed to find the location of the outlaws' camp, but your bravado urged you in closer, so you could get a look at the men responsible for abducting your precious cantor. I'm surprised you haven't attacked the gang already.'

'Keep your voice down,' Scaflock hissed, nervously glancing back at the camp, but he'd misread the situation entirely and he now noticed two more dark shapes appearing from behind the trees as de Flexburgh straightened, a malevolent smile flickering in the nearby firelight.

'Thought you had me nicely locked away, didn't you?' De Flexurgh smiled. 'But the abbot was too stupid to set a proper guard on my cell. When old Brother Walfort came to give me my dinner he forgot to lock the door at his back. He probably doesn't know I'm gone even now, the old lackwit.'

Will brought his sword up as de Flexburgh laughed, and set his feet ready to attack. It was time to show this pitiful excuse for a churchman what it meant to cross Will Scarlet. He braced himself to charge, the thrill of impending battle now coursing through his veins, and then he collapsed on the ground.

Confusion washed over him but he dimly recognised a searing pain in the back of his skull and knew something had hit him. Before he blacked out for the second time in a week, he saw de Flexburgh walking across, teeth glinting.

Will lost consciousness, but not before he'd felt the hated monk's kicks hammering into his body.

Morning came, bright and warm with barely a cloud in the sky, and the sweet sound of a blackbird's song filled the air. As Scaflock opened his eyes, the pain from the previous night's beating washed over him like a bucket of icy water and, hating himself for it, he groaned loudly, curling into a ball with fists and teeth clenched.

'Ah! Our visitor is awake,' an amused voice boomed and Will forced his heavy eyelids open to see who spoke.

It was a filthy looking man of average height but with the build of an ox. His shoulders seemed almost twice as wide as Will's and he wondered if the outlaw's mother had mated with some great beast of the fields rather than a normal man.

'You might as well go back to sleep,' the wolf's head suggested jovially. 'My mates will be back soon, no doubt. I'd offer you some breakfast but I can't be arsed.' The big ox snorted derisively and wandered off, lying down on the grass a short distance away and staring up at the clear blue sky with a contented smile on his round face.

'Jesus, why didn't the bastards just kill me?'

'Because they're frightened of you,' someone replied, and Will, despite the pain, jerked his head around in surprise to look at this other new voice. 'How are your windflowers by the way?'

It was Brother de Loup.

He was tied to a tree but eating again. The sight of the succulent meat being torn apart, juices running down the cantor's lined old face, should have been enough to fire Will's own appetite, but food was the last thing on his mind.

'What? Frightened of me?" Will asked. "Trussed up like a chicken, beaten black and blue? Glad to see you're still alive by the way. Sorry my rescue attempt failed.'

De Loup smiled sadly and spat a piece of bone onto the grass beside him.

'Aye, they know who you are. I made sure to tell them once they'd finished kicking the hell out of you. They decided they didn't want your famous friends like Little John coming after them to avenge your death so they're keeping you alive in hopes of a ransom.'

Will gave a bark of laughter which ended in a howl of pain. He suspected at least one of his ribs might be cracked, possibly more, but at least his reputation had saved him from worse.

'A ransom? For me?'

'Everyone knows you stole a fortune in gold and silver when you were an outlaw.' The cantor nodded, frowning reproachfully back at him. 'I'm quite sure you didn't turn it all over to the abbey when you became a monk – no one ever does! – so it stands to reason you gave it all to your kith and kin.' He shrugged. 'At least, that was Brother de Flexburgh's reasoning once he realised the outlaw leader wasn't going to kill you.'

Will's hands were tied in front of him, and a long, heavy length of rope was looped tightly around his ankles so he'd have no chance of removing it without drawing the attention of their lumbering guard. He lay back as comfortably as he could manage given his bindings and watched a solitary cloud sail slowly across the sky, gathering his thoughts and pushing the pain in his aching body to the back of his mind as he'd learned to do when he was a young mercenary.

'Where the hell are they all then?'

The cantor threw the remnants of his breakfast into the bushes behind him and took a drink from a cup of water that lay beside him.

'Gone to the abbey.'

Again, Will lay in silence for a time, watching the sky, feeling the gentle breeze across his bruised body, letting de Loup's words find a home in his brain.

'The abbey?'

'Aye. Don't you remember?'

He pulled himself up onto his elbows, surprised that it didn't hurt as much as he'd expected.

'Remember what?'

'De Flexburgh seemed to think they hadn't sent all the abbey's treasures along in the ransom. He told the outlaws there was more to be had back at Selby and, well, he's right, isn't he? I didn't see the abbot's golden crook or silver ring in that sack so they must still be in the abbey somewhere, and God knows they are worth a small fortune. And where are the relics? You know we have one of St Damasus's testicles?'

'Only one?' Will demanded, frowning. 'Where's the other one?'

'I don't know.' De Loup waved a hand irritably, as if it wasn't important. 'In Heaven probably.'

'In Heaven? One bollock?'

The cantor ignored his incredulous laugh and continued to piously recite the list of relics held at Selby Abbey.

Will shook his head and tested the bindings around his wrists and ankles, but despair settled upon him like a heavy, sodden cloak. There was no way out – the monks were on their own.

God help them.

* * *

Will had been trying desperately to loosen the ropes around his wrists for what seemed like hours without any success. He now felt surprisingly good, physically, given his beating of the previous evening, but mentally he was suffering terribly.

He'd let everyone in Selby Abbey down, and not only that, he'd placed them all in great danger thanks to his foolish plan.

The outlaws would go through the place like a dose of the runs, killing any who got in their way in their search for the non-existent ransom. And, when they finally realised there was no great prize at the end of their search . . . well, angry outlaws weren't likely to be very merciful.

Again, Will strained his muscles, teeth gritted and beads of sweat standing out on his forehead, but it was no use. The ropes had been bound expertly and so tightly that they were starting to become painful. He thought about asking their oafish guard to loosen them, but one look at the now dozing fellow chased the idea from his mind.

The outlaw would be more likely to smash his boot into Will's face instead of relaxing his bonds. And it was a big boot.

His sword lay on the grass beside the guard, still in its sheath, and Will wished for nothing more than to hold that faithful blade in his hand again. Cold steel would soon set things to rights.

He groaned as a twinge of pain tugged at his neck and the futility of his situation almost overcame him, but the cantor grunted.

'Don't give up hope just yet, Brother Scaflock. Why don't we try praying for God's aid? We are monks after all.'

Will bit back an irritated, sacrilegious retort and shrugged. Why not? A miracle was the only thing that would help them now.

He bowed his head in grudging, beaten assent and closed his eyes, clasping his hands as devoutly as he could manage while the cantor began the Lord's Prayer.

'Pater noster, qui es in caelis: sanctificetur nomen tuum,' Scarlet intoned, surprisingly feeling a sense of calm wash over him. 'Adveniat regnum tuum; fiat voluntas tua.'

The unmistakeable sound of someone approaching broke him from the pious reverie and, tensing his body for the attack he knew must be coming, he opened his eyes.

A shocked grin spread across his face.

'What the hell are you doing here?'

A chipped eating knife began to saw at Will's bonds as he continued to smile like some village idiot. 'I told you to go back to the abbey!'

'I was on my way there when I saw someone on the road ahead,' Brother Nicholas said, returning Will's smile. 'Hid in some bushes until I saw it was de Flexburgh. I knew he must be coming to warn the wolf's heads about you, so . . .'

He shrugged as, at last, his dull blade tore apart the last strand of rope on Will's wrists, and Scaflock reached out to take the blade from him, using it with some ferocity to make short work of the bindings around his ankles.

'I followed him. My limp held me up but their campfire was easy to see.'

'Aye.' Will nodded. 'The idiots should have hid themselves better. Don't suppose they expected some hero from Selby to turn up though!'

Brother Nicholas blushed at the praise and took the knife back from Will's outstretched hand, moving over to remove Brother de Loup's bindings as Scarlet strode across to check on the unmoving guard.

'Good job, lad. This one won't be giving us any trouble for a while.'

Nicholas glanced across, face a mask of concern.

'He'll be all right though, won't he? I hit him with that cudgel you gave me and it worked fine.' He moved back to his task of sawing apart the smiling cantor's bindings while Will examined the fallen outlaw.

The man was quite clearly dead.

'Aye,' Will grunted. 'He'll be fine. You just knocked him out.'

The look of sheer relief on the young monk's face brought a lump to Will's throat, and he was glad he'd lied about the wolf's head's condition.

'We prayed for a miracle,' Brother de Loup suddenly cried out, his hemp shackles now cut free. 'And here he is! Well done, Brother Nicholas. You've saved us.'

Will retrieved his longsword from the grass by the dead outlaw, drawing it from the scabbard to slash the air experimentally.

It felt good, so good, to have it back in his hand again.

'Aye, you saved us,' he agreed. 'But who's going to save the rest of the lads back at the abbey?'

'You,' the cantor said. 'Obviously.'

Will snorted in disbelief.

'Me?'

'Of course.' De Loup nodded, his arms and legs now free of their bindings. He stood up with Nicholas's help, groaning at the tightness in his muscles. 'God sent Brother de Houghton here to send you on your way. That much is clear. You have a sword and can probably take some armour from the downed outlaw. What more do you need?'

'A damn horse would be good,' Will retorted. 'The outlaws have a big head start on me.'

* * *

Brother Robert de Flexburgh was irritated, and not only from the sun which beat down on him as he led the outlaws towards Selby.

He had woken early that morning, nervous excitement making a heavy ball in his stomach. He had exhorted the outlaws to get up and make ready for their visit to the abbey, where they would take the rest of the cantor's ransom money from Abbot de Wystow by force, but the lazy bastards had been too hungover to care for his shouts.

Some had even threatened to cut out his tongue if he didn't shut up.

So he'd held his peace and waited as patiently as he could until the men had forced some food down their gullets and yet more ale to take the edge off their hangovers. Now they plodded along the main road, making no attempt to conceal themselves – why would they? – and their leader, Stephen le Page, grinned at him.

'We'll be wealthy men by the end of this day.'

De Flexburgh nodded, the mention of money raising his spirits. He truly had some horrendous debts that needed to be paid off and, God willing, so they would be after their visit to the abbey.

'What will you do after it?' the wolf's head asked, falling into step beside the tall monk. 'You'll be an outcast. And if things get violent—'

'They will,' someone shouted to gusts of laughter, and le Page grinned back at his friends.

'When things get violent,' he corrected himself, 'you'll be declared an outlaw, just like us. A rich outlaw, granted, but still an outlaw.'

De Flexburgh lowered his eyebrows, not really wanting to think about more violence towards the monks he'd lived with for so long.

'I can speak French,' he replied. 'I'll pay off my gambling debts and sail for Normandy.' He stared ahead at the horizon as they walked, thoughts of the future filling his head. 'An educated man like myself will be able to find a home as a teacher or clerk in some small village by the coast.'

'Wife too, eh?' the outlaw leader leered.

'Nah, he prefers sheep,' one of the others grunted, and the monk found his cheeks burning in anger and embarrassment at the insulting laughter directed his way.

He wasn't used to being laughed at – usually if one of the brothers at the abbey slighted him he'd threaten them or even physically assault them, but he knew he'd have no chance with these men. They were like a pack of wolves – if he attacked one of them, the rest would fall upon him and tear him to pieces.

So he kept silent and contented himself with imagining lightning striking the most abusive ones dead.

Their childish mocking would soon be forgotten once he had his share of the abbot's treasures.

'There it is,' one of the younger outlaws cried, nodding towards the horizon. 'The abbey.'

The men continued walking as the towers of Selby Abbey came closer, and le Page, mouth a grim line now rather than his earlier smile, asked de Flexburgh how he wanted to proceed.

'You're the monk,' the outlaw said. 'You know the place better than us. We can just walk in and start hacking the brothers apart but that seems like a waste of effort.'

'No, no!' De Flexburgh shook his head in alarm. 'We can't do that, for God's sake. I might not think of them all as friends but you can't just go in and murder them all in hopes of finding the ransom.'

'I know,' le Page replied irritably. 'That's why I'm asking you what we should do. Do you know where the valuables will be hidden? Can you lead us to it without too much bloodshed? The last time we were there, some of your brothers fought the mob pretty violently. I'd rather avoid too much direct confrontation if possible. There's only nine of us, after all.'

The wayward monk nodded thoughtfully. He had comrades in the abbey who'd follow his orders, to an extent, and most of the younger monks might not like him but they'd do as they were told too, he was sure. They might not stand by and watch the outlaws ransack the place – again – but they might be persuaded to leave the abbey for a while if de Flexburgh could think of a good enough reason for them to do so . . .

'Right,' he said, a sly smile creeping across his face as he watched a blue tit searching the underside of a branch for tasty insects. 'I've got an idea. Give me some time to see what I can do. If all goes to plan, most – if not all – of the fit and able brothers will soon be out of the way. Conceal yourselves, and come in once they've gone.'

* * *

Will was glad he'd tried to keep fit during his time as a monk. The muscles he'd developed over years as a mercenary and outlaw were still hard beneath his spreading middle-aged bulk, and that had saved him from real, incapacitating damage when the wolf's heads had beaten him the previous night.

He had aches, particularly in his ribs, but he'd drained their dead guard's ale skin, and it had given him a warm glow inside which spurred him on as he jogged towards Selby, wondering what he'd find when he got there.

Would the monks all be dead? Would the grand old building that he now called home be a smoking ruin?

Brother de Houghton and the cantor were following at a much slower pace and Will knew there would be no rescue from his young friend no matter what happened when he reached Selby. Not this time. He was on his own.

Well, not quite, he thought with a savage, lupine grin.

He had his sword.

The dominating spire of Selby Abbey appeared on the horizon and he quickened his pace, the sight of his goal sending a fresh burst of strength through his limbs.

* * *

The abbot and the prior had spent a sleepless night worrying that neither Will nor Nicholas had returned, and where the hell Brother de Flexburgh had disappeared to once his empty cell was discovered. Now de Wystow rubbed his tired eyes and peered out of the small glazed window in his lodging house, which was set a small distance away from the main church, wondering if he was seeing things.

'What's happening? Where's everyone going? Is there a fire?'

Prior Ousthorp looked up from the ledger he was working on, a bemused expression on his face. 'What do you mean?'

'Look,' the abbot said, pointing a thin, wrinkled old digit outside. 'The men are all heading out of the gates.'

Ousthorp rose from his desk and joined his superior at the window. 'There's no fire anyway,' he said with some relief. 'Some of them are laughing. You wait here, I'll go and see what's going on.'

Leaving the abbot, he went outside, locking the door at his back, and walked across the gardens to the south-east, heading for the kitchen where he knew he'd find the bottler. The man was too old to go off wandering around the countryside with the younger monks – Brother Simon Walfort never left the abbey, no matter what. A visit from Satan himself wouldn't be enough to dislodge the bottler from his duties, even if he didn't carry them out quite as mindfully as he was supposed to these days.

No one was on the grounds and the silence seemed eerie as he made his way to his destination, which lay to the south of the cloisters.

'Brother Walfort.' Ousthorp walked into the kitchen and the sight of the elderly bottler washing vegetables reassured him that the last blast of the trumpet wasn't quite as imminent as he'd feared. In saying that, the very Walls of Jericho could be collapsing around him and Brother Walfort would still be preparing dinner.

'What in God's name is happening? Where is everyone going? And why wasn't I informed?'

The old man gave the prior only a cursory, bored glance before he returned to cleaning his carrots.

'Thorp Wyleby. Apparently one of the statues in the church there is crying tears of blood.' The bottler tossed a freshly scrubbed vegetable into a bucket and selected another, which he rubbed a small brush up and down with steady vigour. 'Some of the men have gone to see it.'

'Really?' the prior said, not convinced by the tale. 'Thorp Wyleby is nearly three miles away. I can't see some of our less pious brothers making such a journey on the off-chance they'll see a miracle.'

'You're right,' the bottler grunted. 'Apparently there's a brothel offering cheap rates in the village for pilgrims.'

That made sense to the prior, disgusted as he was. Some of the monks would crawl over Hell's lakes of fire just to spill their filthy seed.

'Who brought news of the miracle?' he demanded.

A new voice broke in then, from the doorway behind the prior.

'I did, Brother.'

Ousthorp turned. It was de Flexburgh.

'And I think it's time we went to see the abbot. Don't you?'

* * *

Will had paced himself well, and by the time he reached the abbey he'd caught his breath and felt quite good, given his bruises and morning's run. He crouched and hurried towards the gates, eyes scanning the roads and area surrounding the entrance for signs of the outlaws.

There were none.

He listened and was pleased not to hear the sounds of men fighting. Had de Flexburgh and his accomplices stopped somewhere on their way here? Or given up on the idea of attacking the abbey again?

Relief gave way to alarm though, as he realised fighting wasn't the only sound he couldn't hear. The grounds outside the building seemed to be utterly devoid of life.

Maybe the monks were all dead!

He restrained himself from charging into the place, sword in hand, and tried to calm his thoughts, to look logically at the situation.

De Flexburgh and his men didn't have that much of a head start on him. They couldn't have wiped out every monk in the abbey by now, surely. Not with such a small force. They'd have met some resistance – many of the monks would have barricaded themselves in rooms with stout doors, and a few of them would even have offered the outlaws some violence of their own.

So what was happening inside the imposing old edifice?

There was only one way to find out.

He leaned out and peered around the side of the gate, eyes searching for signs of anything out of the ordinary. No one was in the gardens so, looking skyward and offering a prayer to God, he held his body low against the ground and sprinted as fast as possible towards the front door of the church, which stood ajar.

When he reached it he stopped, trying to breathe as silently as possible, and listened again, hoping to catch any sound that might offer a clue as to what was going on inside.

Still nothing but that heavy, oppressive silence.

He gripped the hilt of his sword tighter and slipped in through the open doorway, senses straining, alert for any minute sign of danger as he moved through the nave, his eyes jarred as they always were by the sight of the crooked Norman arches which had slipped due to subsidence.

There was a sound then, of wood grinding against wood, and Will recognised it as a drawer being opened. A grunt, then the sound of another drawer being pulled open followed by a disappointed, muttered curse.

Someone was in the chamber to the right – the sacristy. And from the sounds of it, whoever it was had decided to idly search the place for whatever they might find.

It was possible some monk was in there looking for something to steal. Someone like de Flexburgh or one of his friends who had no scruples, for example. But it was far more likely to be one of the outlaws. Probably one of them had been ordered to stand guard at the door while his fellows went on, deeper into the abbey complex, and he'd become bored. Now he was in the sacristy idly hunting for whatever valuables he could carry away.

Will knew the altar goods in that room were worth a great deal, but they were fairly securely locked away and, from the shouted oath he heard now, it seemed the robber had collected little so far. An empty-handed outlaw would be more of a threat than one laden with chalices and crucifixes, so as Will approached the sacristy he moved silently, ready for an attack at any moment.

Just as well.

The robber wore soft boots of leather with soles worn almost completely through, allowing him to move almost as quietly as Will did; oblivious to the threat that was coming for him, he stepped out of the sacristy and spotted Scaflock in the gloom.

Instinctively, the outlaw, a small, wiry man with heavy bags under his eyes and a sweating bald head, flicked his dagger from its place on his belt and threw it.

By the grace of God the missile smashed against Will's hastily drawn sword and clattered uselessly to the floor.

The outlaw knew his business though, and rather than panicking or becoming flustered, he charged directly at Scaflock, intending to crush him against the wall where he could then pummel the winded monk with his bare hands.

Will was ready though, and dodged out of the way so the outlaw barrelled past him at full pelt, slamming against the great stone brickwork and bouncing backwards, directly onto the point of Will's sword. Momentum carried him along the blade, almost to its hilt, and the man stared, wide-eyed, at the mortal wound in his belly, before Will dragged the weapon free in a spray of crimson.

The man swayed for just a moment and then he slumped forward onto his knees, hands clutching desperately at the air as if he might hang onto his ebbing life-force. His fist closed around the wooden rosary Will wore looped into his belt, and the dying man glared accusingly up at him before collapsing onto the ground, rosary snapping in a pattering hail of beads.

'One down,' Will growled, sheathing his sword, which he now realised was too big to fight with effectively inside the narrow corridors of the abbey. 'Only another eight or nine to go.'

* * *

'What do you mean, you don't have the rest of the ransom?' Brother de Flexburgh's voice was tight with fear and anxiety. He'd branded himself a criminal of the worst kind by being part of this mad scheme and now it seemed it hadn't even been worth it.

'Exactly that,' the abbot replied. 'We never did, as you know. It was Brother Scaflock's idea to gather our treasures here in the abbey and send them to the outlaws, to buy the cantor some time.'

'You didn't send *all* your treasures to us though, did you?' Stephen le Page asked, his naturally friendly eyes completely at odds with the hard tone of his words. "That's why we're here. Where's the rest?"

'Gone,' the prior retorted, rubbing his jaw. He'd refused to open the door to the abbot's lodging, but the outlaw leader had punched him and simply taken the key from his pocket before leading the way into the building. 'You thought you were so bloody clever didn't you, de Flexburgh?' Ousthorp spat. 'Cooking up this plan with your criminal friends. But you didn't realise that the de Loup family are not the wealthy lot they were two or three years ago. And' – he shrugged – 'we sent the rest of the abbey's valuables away on a cart to York two days ago to make sure they'd be safe if anything went wrong with Scaflock's plan.'

Abbot de Wystow shook his head, watching his wayward monk sorrowfully. 'You've gone to all this trouble for very little return I'm afraid. Was it worth it, seeing one of your brothers killed by the mob for half a ransom shared out between . . . what?' He looked at the outlaws squeezed into the stifling chamber. 'Seven? Eight men?'

'You're a marked man now,' the prior agreed, but where the abbot wore the expression of a kicked puppy, Ousthorp's eyes blazed with a righteous fury. 'The law, when they finally get here, will be after you, and you can forget about seeking sanctuary anywhere in England. You'll hang for your part in this, as will all your men.'

De Flexburgh's fear was transformed into anger and he lashed out, punching the prior in the cheek, rocking the older man back. To his credit, Ousthorp didn't lose his footing, but simply glared at his attacker from eyes that filled with tears of pain and humiliation at being struck twice by these hateful men.

'That's enough of that,' the abbot cried, finally roused to an emotion stronger than disappointment.

'You're right, it is enough,' the outlaw leader broke in, glaring from the prior to de Flexburgh and then back to the rest of his men. 'The other monks will be back here sooner or later and there's always the possibility someone saw us coming and went to Selby to raise the hue and cry. We need to leave.'

'Empty-handed?' one of the other wolf's heads moaned, and le Page shrugged.

'Go through every room in this whole complex and take whatever gold and silver you can find. I doubt these two' – he jerked his head at the abbot and prior – 'really sent all their treasures to York. They're lying. There's bound to be some choice pieces still dotted about the place. Find them. Go!'

The gang hurried out of the room, jostling one another in their haste to get through the doorway and begin looting.

'Where do they normally keep the valuables, de Flexburgh?' le Page asked, turning back to his traitorous companion, but the tall monk simply shrugged.

The prior shouted an imprecation at le Page, vowing never to tell the man anything, but his eyes grew wide when the outlaw leader drew a wicked-looking dagger and started towards him menacingly.

'Upstairs,' Abbot de Wystow sighed, shaking his head irritably at the prior. 'They'll find it eventually, John. Telling them now will just get them out of here sooner and leave you with all your fingers intact.'

'Exactly.' Le Page grinned. 'It's easier – and safer – to be helpful. Now, I was told you have a nice staff of office amongst other fine treasures. There's no way you'd have sent something as personal as that away on a wagon.' He turned and gestured grandly towards the door. 'Lead me to it, Father Abbot.'

* * *

Will heard the men coming and only just had time to throw himself through the doorway into the eastern cloister before he was spotted. He slipped into the first room he came to – the parlour – and pressed himself into an alcove, listening to the outlaws' movements.

Some of them must have gone off in the opposite direction, which was just as well as Scaflock would never have been able to take them all on at once.

The main babble of voices faded but – from the sounds of footsteps and loud, excited chatter – two other wolf's heads were heading straight for him.

Drawing in a deep breath, Will waited until the first of the approaching men came through into the cloister from the south transept before he burst out, the tip of his dagger aimed at the shocked robber's heart.

The outlaws reacted to his attack instinctively, halting their advance and throwing weapons up with small exclamations of alarm. Will felt a thrill of panic course through him as his short blade was deflected by the leather bracer on his target's wrist, but his momentum carried the point forward inexorably, up and into the outlaw's neck.

The man's alarmed squeal turned to a gurgle of agonised despair as his windpipe was torn through, but Will was too experienced to allow himself to slow. He left the dagger where it had lodged and turned, grasping the second man's wrist and twisting it with brutal strength. The outlaw roared in pain but couldn't stop his natural, instinctual response, which was to fold under the pressure, seeking to release the bone-breaking force.

When he went down Will smashed his knee into the outlaw's face, watching it bounce like a child's ball against the heavy parlour door, then he repeated the move while continuing to twist the arm.

There was a crack of bone and the arm went limp. So did the man, knocked unconscious, although whether from the head trauma or the terrible pain in his arm Will didn't know, or care.

He retrieved his dagger from the dead outlaw's throat and crouched breathlessly, watching and listening for the sound of the downed men's companions running to see what the commotion was all about.

The thick stone walls and massive old wooden doors must have muffled the sounds of the fight and Will let out a long sigh of relief, eyes falling to his defeated opponents. Grabbing the dead outlaw, he hauled the man into the parlour by the feet.

He dropped the corpse and went back out, peering warily along the cloister, then dragged the other outlaw in and shut the door. The man was still alive but Will – a monk now, after all – couldn't bring himself to kill him. Instead, he found a dusty old tablecloth and tore it into strips which he used to bind the man's arms and mouth.

Coughing, and feeling somewhat guilty at the agony he knew the unconscious outlaw would suffer upon waking, Will slipped back out into the corridor and made his way around to the western side of the covered walkway, eyes and ears straining for signs of the other, remaining invaders.

He stopped at the gatehouse and, to its left, the abbot's two-storey lodging house came into view through the unglazed cloister windows. He crouched, pressing himself against the wall and peering out across the grass.

Suddenly, through a narrow tower window of the abbot's building, Will spotted movement. At first he couldn't see who it was as they moved up the stairs but, across the silent, open grounds, he could hear their voices. The outlaw captain le Page's hard tones were instantly recognisable, and his promise to kill the abbot and prior if they didn't find valuables soon chilled Scaflock to the marrow.

The small party passed the window, then the red, anxious face of Brother de Flexburgh looked out momentarily before the tall monk continued upstairs behind his leader and their prisoners.

The warrior monk knew he could take le Page and he'd already bested de Flexburgh without much trouble, so he began to sneak along the airy walkway, intending to head out through the nave where he might use the main walls as cover to allow him to reach the abbot's lodgings without being seen. Then he would simply take out the two ringleaders and hopefully put an end to this entire nightmare.

'Stephen! Stephen!'

Someone was running towards him from the direction of the priory, and Will had to sprint out into the nave, where he threw himself behind the supporting column known as Abbot Hugh's pillar, with its carved diamond pattern.

'Patrick's dead! I found him in a room near the door where we left him standing guard. Someone's in the abbey with us!'

The alarmed man's voice dropped in pitch as he ran past and headed outside across the grounds, but Will could still hear the conversation clearly enough as le Page went back to the tower window he'd just passed and shouted out, demanding to know what his companion was babbling about.

'Where's Gareth and Malcolm the Mouth? Didn't you pass them on your way here?' The outlaw leader sounded confused and tense, almost shouting now. 'They headed into the cloister at the far end, I saw them go myself. Oh, in the name of . . . Wait there, I'm coming down.'

Will knew it was time to move again before he was discovered, and he ran towards the north porch and out through the door, blinking in the sunlight as he made his way swiftly around to the gardens outside the choir, where he lost himself amongst some bushes.

He couldn't hear much now but he could imagine what was happening inside the abbey. Le Page and his companion would have discovered their dead and injured friends and must now be alerting the rest of the outlaws to his murderous presence.

The element of surprise had gone.

They knew he was coming for them, but he couldn't stay out here in the bushes – it wasn't in his nature to hide for long.

He had to rest for a time however, and regain his breath, so he leaned back against the thick foliage and stared straight ahead, feeling a sense of calm settle over him, his heart returning to its usual, steady beat. A soft murmur escaped his lips as he sent a prayer heavenwards, begging the Lord's assistance and protection for the abbot.

The outlaws wouldn't leave just because they knew someone was stalking them – they'd continue their search for gold and loot but they'd move in pairs or packs now, and they'd be expecting him to appear at any moment. He'd need to use everything, every skill in his personal armoury, to come out of this in one piece, never mind save Abbot de Wystow.

Grinning savagely, feeling more alive than he'd done in years, he crept slowly back towards the north door, absently noting the strange carving of a monk in a ship on the wall high above. It was Selby Abbey's founder, the French monk Benedict who had come to England with the dried finger of St Germain almost three hundred years earlier.

Will didn't have the miraculous finger of a revered saint to help him that day, but his knife would do just as well.

* * *

He could hear the sounds of things being thrown – drawers and other storage no doubt – as he moved back through the nave, bloody dagger still held tightly in his hand. He guessed that meant a couple of the gang were searching one of the rooms for booty while another stood guard. The problem was, it sounded like it was coming from the priory, which only had one entrance and was reached via the cloister with nowhere to hide.

They would see him coming.

He wondered what to do. Should he leave those outlaws to whatever they were up to and search for a different target? Was it a trap they'd laid for him, so when he appeared, more of the gang would attack him from behind?

If only he had someone to watch his back.

Will had never been one to turn away from a challenge though. Quite the opposite in fact, he'd often got himself into danger by acting rashly, through bravado or anger.

'Why change the habits of a lifetime?' he murmured, walking purposefully towards the priory.

Anxious shouts came to him before he re-entered the cloister leading towards his destination, and he guessed the searchers had found little or nothing of value. He looked along the corridor and saw one lookout at the far end.

The fool had his back to Will, presumably watching his enraged fellows, so the vengeful monk took his chance, running along the cloister as fast as he could without his sandals making too much noise.

He wasn't fast enough though, and the outlaw turned, spotting Scaflock before he could launch an attack.

'He's here!' the lookout cried, bringing up his sword and using it to jab at Will. The narrow, enclosing walls left no room for a swing, and the clumsy lunge was easily sidestepped by Will, who barrelled into the wolf's head, ramming him against the solid door surround with his shoulder and plunging his dagger into the man's belly.

Once, twice, again, and this time he used his great strength to drag the blade up, creating the biggest wound he could, then, knowing it was a mortal blow, he leaned back, raised his leg and kicked the dying outlaw in through the doorway, just in time to hit one of his oncoming comrades.

Will had guessed right – there had been two other wolf's heads in the priory. One was momentarily stunned by the body of his friend, but the other roared a curse and threw himself at Will.

This one didn't make the same mistake as his companion, didn't lunge with his sword – instead he brought it round for a powerful swing, but the blade was too long and it bounced back from the wall with a clang and a small shower of sparks. The attacker screamed as pain lanced like fire along his arm and into his shoulder, which Will thought might have dislocated.

The final outlaw had shoved his now-dead friend aside and came forward, eyeing his surviving companion who was gasping in agony and holding his injured shoulder with a look on his pale face that suggested he might pass out at any moment.

'You know who I am,' Will stated in a low, strong voice. 'And you can see why the minstrels sing songs about me now, eh?' The outlaw blanched but gritted his teeth and held his sword up, setting his legs in a defensive stance. 'That's five of your mates I've dealt with now. Six, if you count that big arsehole you left at the campsite to guard me.'

The wolf's head with the dislocated shoulder slumped to the floor just then, and Will grinned wickedly.

'Come on, boy. Be a part of the minstrels' next song about me.'

The outlaw was young, clearly inexperienced and quite terrified. He turned and ran back inside the priory towards the small adjoining chapel, stopping only for a moment to try and slam the door shut before realising his deceased friend was blocking the entrance.

Will knew the priory was a dead end, so the beardless lad had nowhere to run to.

He glanced down at the corpse in the doorway and noticed the key still in the lock. That was handy – almost a miracle in fact, as he knew the monks usually didn't leave the key there. Maybe the outlaws had taken it from someone? Whatever the explanation, Will silently offered a prayer of thanks to God and kicked the dead outlaw out of the way. He'd rather not fight the boy unless he had to, and he also had no desire to kill the injured fellow on the floor. Instead, he dragged that one inside the chamber, as the frightened youngster watched him from behind the altar of the chapel. Then he went out and closed the door.

With a satisfying click he turned the key in the lock and put it into a pocket inside his robe.

The door was thick and the lock a good one. It would hold the prisoners for a time – long enough at least for Will to finish off the last of their bastard companions.

He hoped . . .

* * *

'What are we going to do?' de Flexburgh demanded, a taut spring of nervous, frightened energy, and his outlaw companion glared in disgust at him.

'Shut your mouth for a start,' le Page growled. 'Panicking will do us no favours. Even if this crazy monk manages to evade our men, we still have these two as hostages.'

The abbot looked tired but the prior's face was still angry.

'You'd be better just getting your backsides out of here right now,' he muttered, glaring at his captors. 'Scaflock has a well-earned reputation for violence. He's already killed some of your men and I'm sure he'll be along any moment to end this for good.'

Le Page laughed. 'You think so? I doubt it. Now that we know he's here, my lads will deal with him easily enough. He might have had a name years ago but he's a fat old monk now and we still have him outnumbered by about six to one.'

'Two to one you mean.'

The big outlaw captain spun, his mouth dropping open at the sight of Will standing in the open doorway, not a scratch on him.

'I've killed all your friends,' Scarlet growled, eyes burning with a frightening intensity, and he felt a pang of guilt at the exaggeration as the abbot blanched, sickened by the thought of so much death within his abbey.

'You low-born sack of dog shit!' de Flexburgh shouted, his fear transformed into rage at the sight of the man who'd wrecked his carefully laid plans. The wayward monk drew a sharp-looking knife from inside his black robe and lunged across the room, grabbing Prior Ousthorp and placing the blade against the older man's neck. 'Get out of here, Scaflock. Get the hell out of here now or I'll kill him.'

Will wasn't sure what to do. The dangerous-looking outlaw leader was watching him with a steely glare, muscles taut, ready to strike just as soon as he saw an opening, and Will could tell this one would be much harder to defeat in a straight fight than any of the other filth he'd bested that day. As they locked gazes, le Page's eyes flickered almost imperceptibly to a point outside the room.

At the same instant there was a grunt of exertion from behind, but Will had read and understood the signs and the sword-point that was meant for his back pierced nothing but thin air.

As silent as a cat, Scaflock had dodged to the side and now brought his own dagger around, feeling it slam home in this new assailant's body. Before he could continue his attack though, from the corner of his eye Will saw le Page coming for him and, again, he had to throw his body to the side to avoid being spitted like a piece of beef.

He threw a punch, felt it hit home in le Page's face, and the man stumbled in his lunge, falling against the door awkwardly, knife falling to the floor with a clatter. Will tried to follow it up by plunging his dagger into the man, but the outlaw he'd stabbed flailed his legs, tripping him, to a shout of alarm from the abbot.

Will slashed wildly with his dagger, once again feeling it bite home, and prayed he'd killed the maggot as he managed to regain his feet, but with a roar of animal fury le Page grabbed him, using his momentum to force Scaflock backwards. Their legs became entangled, and both men ended up on the floor once more, teeth bared, grappling for their very lives.

Will felt the back of his head bounce off the stone and a flare of panic ran through him. Again he felt his opponent's hand on his throat and again his skull hit the floor, making sparks of light explode in his vision.

Le Page knew he had his victory now, and he channelled all his energy into continuing that one, murderous attack, eyes widening with joyous battle fever, the desire to see Scaflock's tonsured head split like an egg filling him with a terrible, almost carnal need.

Despite his massive, bull-like neck, Will couldn't withstand the outlaw's grasping hand. He was weak – tired after fighting so many outlaws and his forced run that morning.

As his head hit the floor for a third time he heard the abbot screaming, and even the prior shouted at le Page to stop in an anguished voice, but there would be no quarter given from this outlaw, Will knew.

His hands were trapped underneath le Page's heavy body, but as he was battered unconscious, he remembered the dagger he held, and twisted his fist, feeling only hard pressure against the blade as it met the outlaw's chainmail.

Desperately, blackness filling his head, he forced his dagger round and upwards, pushing against his opponent's armour.

And then the pressure was gone as the blade found a space between the mail links and the weight crushing down on him fell away.

'What have you done to me?'

Le Page's voice was high-pitched and hysterical but Will couldn't move to see what the wolf's head was talking about.

'Oh, Jesus, Christ above,' de Flexburgh muttered from somewhere far away, the renegade monk's voice betraying a note of hysteria. 'You've killed him! You've killed them all, you bastard, but now – I'll kill you!'

* * *

Prior Ousthorp sat on the floor, a shocked look on his face, hands trembling as he tried to take in the day's events.

Abbot de Wystow slumped down next to him, the nervous energy that had kept him upright for so long dissipating now.

'So much violence . . . so much death in my own abbey .
. .'

It was all over, and hopefully the rest of the monks would return soon to help deal with the aftermath of de Flexburgh's twisted scheme. The broken furniture, the smashed doors. The bloody corpses including that of their own brother.

The abbot gazed at the black-robed body on the floor of his chamber and shook his head sorrowfully.

'How did we let things get this far?' he murmured. 'Was I really too lenient with the brothers, as Archbishop Melton said? Could I have done things differently?'

For a moment there was silence, the old stones of the abbey dispassionately taking in his words, and then a groan filled the room and the prior jerked fearfully.

'Help him, John,' de Wystow shouted, face lighting with hope. 'Hurry!'

Will opened his eyes and saw the prior bending over him but, before he could speak, he rolled onto his side and vomited. When he was finished he squeezed his eyes shut and gave a small squeal of pain. It felt like the worst hangover he'd ever experienced, and the prior's half-hearted attempt to comfort him with a patting hand did little to ease his discomfort.

'What happened?' he mumbled through wet lips. 'Why didn't de Flexburgh finish me off?' He tried to focus and squinted in surprise as he took in the sight of the tall monk's body on the ground just yards away, a red patch matting the side of his head.

'You can thank Abbot de Wystow for your life,' Ousthorp replied. 'When de Flexburgh let him go to come after you, the abbot lifted that brass candelabra and smashed it off the big oaf's head.'

'Quite a weight in it,' de Wystow opined. 'I only meant to stun him but . . .'

Will moved onto all fours, panting and pressing a hand against the back of his own head, which was bloody but didn't seem cracked, despite the pain that assailed him.

'God lent strength to your arm,' he said, retrieving his dropped dagger before finally hauling himself to his feet and glancing slowly around the room.

The outlaw leader, Stephen le Page, had a terrible gaping wound just above his genitals where Will's blade had pierced the mail and torn deeply through the man's flesh. It wouldn't have killed instantly but it had been enough to throw le Page back in mortal fear, saving Will from having his head bashed in.

The other wolf's head, the one who'd sneaked up behind him, had a similar crimson wound but it was in the side of his head, and Scaflock recalled lashing out blindly, hoping to land a killing blow.

'Lock the door,' he grunted, leaning against the wall as his head began to spin again. 'Hurry, prior. I didn't really kill all the outlaws – some of them are still alive, locked away. They might get out and come for us and I'm in no state to fight again. Although' – he forced a sickly smile onto his face – 'from the looks of Brother de Flexburgh, the abbot and his candelabra can deal with any more of the whoresons that might turn up.'

With that, he slumped to the ground and passed out again.

* * *

It took a few days for Will to recover most of his strength, although even then the abbot ordered him to stay indoors on light duties. Peeling carrots was no work for him however, and he was utterly fed up by the time the abbey had been visited by the bailiff and things were back to normal.

The other monks had returned to the abbey a few hours after Will collapsed, and word had been sent to Selby. A request for aid was sent – again – to the sheriff in Nottingham, but in the meantime the tithing had been called out and the men of Selby came to the abbey that evening, led by the headman James Kay.

The outlaws Will had locked away were still where he'd left them, a testament to the quality of the old locks, and the men had gone quietly enough once they knew there was no chance of escape. In truth, they'd been hungry, tired, and just grateful to have survived an encounter with the legendary Will Scarlet.

He felt far from legendary though, when he'd collapsed again and found himself confined to the hard bed in the dormitory. The damage to his skull might not have killed him but it would take some time to recover from it.

Time he knew he'd spend mostly alone.

The monks viewed him as a God-sent hero, particularly the cantor, who, slowed by his ordeal, returned safely with Brother de Houghton the day after the invasion. Will had thought the adulation amusing at first but now it irritated him – the brothers meant well but they didn't see him as a man. To them he was some kind of avenging angel. Even Nicholas looked at him with awe when he visited his bedside which, strangely, made Will feel lonelier than ever before.

The abbot and prior were both grateful for what he'd done but he knew for sure now that he didn't belong in the abbey. Recent events had proved that beyond a doubt.

What kind of monk maimed and killed so many men, even to help his brothers?

He tried to pray. To be pious. But the fact was, Will simply wasn't that impressed with God. Where had God been when his wife and children – even his dog! – were slaughtered all those years ago?

But where else could he go? His life was at a dead end, just as it had been all those months before when he'd first come – lost – to the abbey. No one wanted a used-up old mercenary with a bad temper.

The cantor came in one morning, a broad smile on his face which Will didn't even attempt to return.

'I've got a surprise for you,' de Loup said, a twinkle in his eyes. 'We all know you're not truly happy here.'

Will grunted irritably at the cantor's words.

'Why are you smiling about it then, if you know how I feel?'

De Loup's grin never wavered, in fact it grew wider as he looked out into the corridor and waved a hand, beckoning whoever was out there to come into the small bedchamber.

Will tore his glare away from the cantor, eyeing the doorway as someone came in and, on seeing who it was, he broke into the widest smile anyone in Selby had ever seen on his face.

'Beth,' he breathed. 'It's good to see you, lass. What brings you here?'

'Come to see you, you old fool,' she scowled, and the cantor raised his eyebrows, shocked at the girl's disrespect, but Will laughed and waved the old man away.

It was good to be spoken to like a man for a change, instead of a hero.

Beth came across and sat on the bed next to her father as the cantor closed the door quietly behind him.

She leaned forward and peered into his eyes, then inspected the back of his head. 'Are you all right? Truly? The abbot sent word to us and it sounded like you were badly injured.' Before he could answer she continued in a furious hiss, eyes wet. 'What the hell were you thinking? You're not a twenty-five-year-old soldier any more, Da!'

'I know that,' he retorted. 'Only too well. But I managed to save my friends and stop those outlaw bastards, didn't I? I'm not completely useless just yet, despite what everyone might think.'

His tone surprised Beth, and her expression softened as she grasped his hand.

'No one thinks you're useless. Since when did self-pity become one of your problems?'

Will sighed and forced a small, rueful smile onto his face.

'Why are you here?' he asked again. 'I mean, it's nice to see you, but you have your own duties at home. Especially now you have a son of your own.'

'Are you happy living here?'

The question took him aback completely and he looked away, at the floor, unsure how to answer. He and his daughter had been close, even despite the period when she'd been taken and used as a servant by a rich nobleman while Will thought her dead. But he'd never been one for talking about his feelings.

'Are you?' the girl demanded, squeezing his hand and gazing at him earnestly. 'Tell me the truth. I was shocked when you said you were coming here to become a monk, but you had your reasons and I respected them. Now though . . .'

'What?' he asked.

'The abbot's message said you didn't belong here. No!' she almost shouted, raising her hands in the air. 'He didn't mean it like that – he doesn't want rid of you. The monks just don't think you're happy here, although they all love you. Who wouldn't?' She grinned disarmingly. 'With your jovial nature and easy smile?'

'Watch it – you're not too big for a clip around the ear,' Will groused, but his empty threat only made her smile wider.

Neither of them said anything for a while but Beth stared at him, waiting on an answer to her question.

'No,' Will finally muttered. 'I'm not happy here. I like some of the monks well enough but . . . I'm bored. I feel like my time could be used better somewhere else.'

'Where?'

'I don't know,' he admitted. 'I stopped those outlaws and it felt good, but I don't want to spend the rest of my days fighting. Or praying,' he ended quietly, shrugging his broad shoulders and sinking back into his bedding with a bleak expression. 'From one extreme to the other . . .'

'Come home with me.'

Will didn't think he'd heard her right. Thought his damaged head had imagined her words. He looked at her, wishing she'd really said it.

'Come home with me,' Beth repeated. 'Please. Robert needs his grandfather.'

Tears filled his eyes at the idea of being with his beloved daughter again, and at hearing the name of his grandson, named after his old friend Robin Hood who Will missed terribly.

'You don't need me around,' he mumbled, fearing his voice would break. 'You have your own family now.'

'And you're part of it – you always will be.' Beth got to her feet and bent to kiss his forehead. 'I never wanted you to leave Wakefield in the first place but I didn't want to stand in your way when you said you would become a Benedictine. Now, though . . . You have friends at home who miss you. Tuck, Little John, Elspeth.' She placed her hands on her hips and glared at him, looking so much like her long-dead mother that Will's breath caught in his throat. 'You're coming home with me.'

With that, she swept from the room and he could hear her conversing outside with the cantor.

He allowed the tears to spill from his eyes, a maelstrom of emotions and memories filling him, but the main, overarching feeling was joy.

He was going home.

Epilogue

Come back, you bastard, I'll kill you!'

For a time he was too angry to notice the men watching him from the other side of the fence. He'd been trying to herd the flock of sheep for a while now but one of the woolly clods wouldn't do as he ordered, infuriating him so much he almost felt like going inside and finding his old sword. Mutton stew seemed a good idea right then.

Finally the beast stood still long enough for the farmer to catch it and haul it into the pen, ready to have its thick coat sheared. He struggled with the animal for a time but finally harvested most of its soft bounty and shooed the beast back into the field with a tired sigh.

'Good job.'

Will Scaflock spun at the voice, face red with anger, sensing the sarcasm in the words and ready to deliver a vicious retort of his own.

His face broke into a wide grin though, when he saw who his visitors were.

'Brother de Loup. Nicholas. Good to see you – it's been a long time! Come on. That lot' – he nodded breathlessly towards the penned sheep – 'can wait a bit. Share an ale with me.'

They went into the farmhouse, and a small boy no more than three years old ran to meet them, looking warily up at the tonsured newcomers.

Will patted the lad's shoulder with reassuring words and sent him outside to play, the love in his eyes shining like a beacon on a dark night. He poured three mugs of ale and set them down on the table in the middle of the small room beside a freshly baked loaf, gesturing at his visitors to help themselves.

'You've allowed your own hair to grow back,' the cantor noted, reaching for his mug. 'Probably just as well – you never suited a tonsure.'

'Nobody suits a tonsure,' Will laughed with a raised eyebrow. 'What brings you here?'

De Loup smiled, and smacked his lips in satisfaction as he tasted the ale. 'We just wanted to see how you fared now that you're back home in Wakefield.'

Brother Nicholas nodded agreement, stuffing a piece of bread into his mouth happily. 'Aye! How are you?'

'Couldn't be happier.' Will smiled, and the truth of it was plain in his voice. 'My daughter is an incredible young woman.'

Just then the child burst back in through the doorway, a tiny ball of wild motion. He grabbed Will's hand and, laughing loudly, tried to drag him onto the floor.

'Not just now, Robert.' The one-time outlaw grinned. 'I have important visitors.'

The boy wouldn't give up however, and continued to pull at Will's hand, his smile widening but nearing the point where it might soon turn into a petulant temper tantrum.

The cantor looked sideways at Brother Nicholas, both of the monks preparing for the explosion of anger they expected at any second, but their former colleague surprised them completely by allowing himself to be dragged onto the rushes that carpeted the floor.

'Ah!' Will cried out, curling up in mock pain while his tiny grandson clambered on top of him and slapped his muscular arms, laughing the whole time as if he'd burst with the fun of it all.

'Stop! Stop, I beg you! I've had enough.'

The little boy continued his assault for a while, then, bored at last, jumped off his victim and ran back outside, still shrieking with laughter. His grandfather rose and regained his seat beside the monks, apparently not embarrassed at all by the straw in his hair or the general unruly state of him after his 'beating' at the hands of the wild infant.

'I'm glad to see you're enjoying life to the fullest again,' the cantor said. 'Your brothers in Selby send their best wishes and they'll be happy to hear our report when we return home. We would have visited sooner but it's a fair journey, as you know.'

'All is well with you though?' Nicholas asked. 'Truly?'

'Truly.' Will nodded. 'I don't care overmuch for the farm – I gave it to Beth when I went to Selby after all – but I get to spend a lot of time with young Robert there and, well, you saw him. He's taken years off me.' He sipped his ale, smiling contentedly. 'And Beth has been so good to me since I came back here. A man couldn't ask any more from his daughter. Little John and Tuck have even visited a few times too – I think Beth must have told them I needed a friend. We've had a few drunken nights out at the local alehouse, let me tell you . . .'

The three men sat in companionable silence for a time, enjoying the simple yet tasty food and drink on Will's table until, eventually, Nicholas asked the question that had also been playing on the cantor's mind.

'What happens when the little lad is grown and . . . ?'

It was a fair question. The monks assumed he might feel lonely and lost again once Robert was a few years older and didn't need his grandfather to play with anymore.

Just then Robert's voice could be heard squealing in excitement, and a woman's friendly tones replied, the sound approaching and growing louder until, at last, a face peered in at the men.

'Grandpa, Elspeth is here!'

Robert tore into the house again then stared up at Will. 'I need a drink.'

The men laughed and Will handed the lad a cup of watered-down ale, shooing him away, back outside.

When he had gone all eyes returned to the open doorway. A tall, pretty lass of near thirty years carrying a small bunch of white, musky-smelling flowers stood there shyly.

'Come on in, Elspeth.' Will smiled, gesturing her forward. 'These are friends of mine from the abbey.'

Nicholas in particular eyed the newcomer with clear appreciation, drinking in the sight of her clear white skin, freshly combed brown hair and . . .

Will laughed at the young monk's surprise.

'Aye.' He nodded, taking the girl's hand and drawing her in beside him. 'Friar Tuck married us in the spring and I'm to be a father again.' He patted her swollen belly lovingly. 'And I – we – couldn't be happier. I'll be a busy man for a while yet. Does that answer your last question?'

AUTHOR'S NOTE

So, this is it: the final book in the Forest Lord series. I always liked Will Scarlet as a character – he seemed to have a lot going on in his head and the thought that he might have ended up becoming a monk really interested me. We all change as we get older, after all, and I wondered how Will would take to life in an abbey, given his legendary temper. It had to be a fun tale, right? Hopefully it was.

Readers might be surprised to know The Abbey of Death is, somewhat, based on real events. I didn't know this when I started writing it, but, as so often seems to happen to an author, research throws up facts that really help shape a story. In this case, I was eating my breakfast on the day I was to start writing and I was flicking through Terry Jones's Medieval Lives when I read about the troubles at Bury St Edmunds Abbey in 1327. Apparently 3,000 townsfolk had attacked the place because they were sick of the monks' loose living. I looked into it a little more on the Internet, wondering if anywhere closer to Will Scaflock's home in Wakefield might have had similar problems.

Sure enough, Selby Abbey, a little over twenty miles away, had been blessed with wicked clergymen just like those in Bury St Edmunds, and it became clear I could use this to flesh out what had been, until that point, a rather basic outline for the planned novella.

The monks at Selby were pretty naughty back then, to the extent that Archbishop Melton censured the real Abbot

John de Wystow II on more than one occasion. Monks like Adam de la Breuer, Thomas de Hirst, John de Whitgift, and, of course, Robert de Flexburgh were guilty of a variety of transgressions: gossiping; sending alms to 'a certain suspected woman'; 'incontinence with certain women of the town'; and general lascivious, dissolute behaviour.

So you might have read The Abbey of Death thinking it was all a bit far-fetched but, in truth, I toned things down. Medieval monks were often nothing like the softly spoken, thoughtful Cadfael from the TV show – many were hard bastards who liked a good drink and a night with a prostitute. Some of whom actually wandered openly around the cloisters in Bury St Edmunds!

Who would have thought Will Scarlet would take exception to such behaviour? I think the Will we saw in Wolf's Head might have accepted it easily enough, but he's older, wiser and, I believe, a better man in this novella thanks to his experiences with Robin Hood's gang.

A couple of little things I should note: as pointed out by my excellent beta reader Nicky Galliers, the lowly monks would not have retained their family names, but I felt it would have been a chore for readers if I only called, for example, de Flexburgh, 'Brother Robert' all the time; secondly, I have taken a few liberties with the layout of Selby Abbey to make the action a little more exciting. There doesn't seem to be a ground plan of the original buildings, much of which were destroyed by fire in 1340.

I hope you enjoyed the tale and will continue to follow my work as I move on from these well-loved characters and begin to create my own new ones, starting with Bellicus the druid in post-Roman Britain. I'm having a fine time with him, and his supporting cast, and I hope to have his first adventure ready to publish around summer/autumn of this year (2017).

Have a great summer, readers, and as always, thank you for your support!

Steven A. McKay
Old Kilpatrick
30 March 2017

If you enjoyed The Abbey of Death, please take a moment to leave a review on Amazon, Goodreads etc. and let others know what you thought. Even just a short line or two is a huge help and I appreciate (and read) every one of them.

To receive another, completely FREE, short story, take a moment to sign up for my mailing list. VIP subscribers will get exclusive access to giveaways, competitions, and info on new releases. Just head to the link below to sign up. As a thank you, you'll be automatically emailed my exclusive story 'The Rescue' which features more of my Forest Lord characters.

https://stevenamckay.com/mailing-list/
Facebook: www.facebook.com/RobinHoodNovel
Official website: stevenamckay.com/
And on Twitter, follow @SA_McKay

THANK YOU FOR READING!

ACKNOWLEDGEMENTS

Thank you to my beta readers, Bernadette McDade and Nicky Galliers, who helped me out a lot, particularly with the religious and historical aspects of the story. The fine people at Selby Abbey, particularly John Weetman, sent me some really useful stuff to help with my research, for which I am most grateful.

A huge and probably overdue thanks to my editor, Richenda Todd. She has edited every one of my novels and novellas so far (not copy-edited, I should add – all mistakes there are mine!), really allowing me to see any flaws in the early drafts and making the entire series the best it could be.

Thank you to the people at Amazon Publishing for making *The Abbey of Death* my first professionally/traditionally (as opposed to self) published book!

Finally, I couldn't close out the Forest Lord series without mentioning my children, Freya, Riley, and Lianna, who inspire me every day. I love you!

Printed in Great Britain
by Amazon

44759013R00069